CHILDREN'S
CLASSICS

THE STRANGE CASE OF
DR JEKYLL AND MR HYDE
&
THE SUICIDE CLUB

Robert Louis Stevenson

D1303362

Bloomsbury Books
London

This edition published 1994 by Bloomsbury Books, an imprint
of The Godfrey Cave Group, 42 Bloomsbury Street, London,
WC1B 3QJ.

ISBN 1 85471 222 5

Printed and bound by Firmin-Didot (France),
Group Herissey. No d'impression : 27113.

Contents

THE STRANGE CASE OF DR JEKYLL AND MR HYDE

THE SUICIDE CLUB

1

Story of the Door

Mr Utterson the lawyer was a man of a rugged countenance, that was never lighted by a smile; cold, scanty, and embarrassed in discourse; backward in sentiment; lean, long, dusty, dreary, and yet somehow lovable. At friendly meetings, and when the wine was to his taste, something eminently human beaconed from his eye; something indeed which never found its way into his talk, but which spoke not only in these silent symbols of the after-dinner face, but more often and loudly in the acts of his life. He was austere with himself; drank gin when he was alone, to mortify a taste for vintages; and though he enjoyed the theatre, had not crossed the doors of one for twenty years. But he had an approved tolerance for others, sometimes wondering, almost with envy, at the high pressure of spirits involved in their misdeeds, and in any extremity inclined to help rather than to reprove. "I incline to Cain's heresy," he used to say quaintly; "I let my brother go to the devil in his own way." In this character, it was frequently his fortune to be the last reputable acquaintance and the last good influence in the lives of down-going men. And to such as these, so long as they came about his chambers, he never marked a shade of change in his demeanour.

No doubt the feat was easy to Mr Utterson; for he

was undemonstrative at the best, and even his friend-
ships seemed to be found in a similar catholicity of
good-nature. It is the mark of a modest man to accept
his friendly circle ready-made from the hands of opportunity; and that was the lawyer's way. His friends
were those of his own blood, or those whom he had
known the longest; his affections, like ivy, were the
growth of time, they implied no aptness in the object.
Hence, no doubt, the bond that united him to Mr
Richard Enfield, his distant kinsman, the well-known
man about town. It was a nut to crack for many, what
these two could see in each other, or what subject they
could find in common. It was reported by those who
encountered them in their Sunday walks, that they said
nothing, looked singularly dull, and would hail with
obvious relief the appearance of a friend. For all that, the
two men put the greatest store by these excursions,
counted them the chief jewel of each week, and not only
set aside occasions of pleasure, but even resisted the calls
of business, that they might enjoy them uninterrupted.

It chanced on one of these rambles that their way led
them down a by-street in a busy quarter of London.
The street was small and what is called quiet, but it
drove a thriving trade on the week-days. The inhabit-
ants were all doing well, it seemed, and all emulously
hoping to do better still, and laying out the surplus of
their gains in coquetry, so that the shop fronts stood
along that thoroughfare with an air of invitation, like
rows of smiling saleswomen. Even on Sunday, when it
veiled its more florid charms and lay comparatively
empty of passage, the street shone out in contrast to its
dingy neighbourhood, like a fire in a forest; and with
its freshly painted shutters, well-polished brasses, and

general cleanliness and gaiety of note, instantly caught and pleased the eye of the passenger.

Two doors from one corner, on the left hand going east, the line was broken by the entry of a court; and just at that point, a certain sinister block of building thrust forward its gable on the street. It was two stories high; showed no window, nothing but a door on the lower story and a blind forehead of discoloured wall on the upper; and bore in every feature the marks of prolonged and sordid negligence. The door, which was equipped with neither bell nor knocker, was blistered and distained. Tramps slouched into the recess and struck matches on the panels; children kept shop upon the steps; the schoolboy had tried his knife on the mouldings; and for close on a generation, no one had appeared to drive away these random visitors or to repair their ravages.

Mr Enfield and the lawyer were on the other side of the by-street, but when they came abreast of the entry, the former lifted up his cane and pointed.

"Did you ever remark that door?" he asked; and when his companion had replied in the affirmative, "It is connected in my mind," added he, "with a very odd story."

"Indeed !" said Mr Utterson, with a slight change of voice, "and what was that ?"

"Well, it was this way," returned Mr Enfield: "I was coming home from some place at the end of the world, about three o'clock of a black winter morning, and my way lay through a part of town where there was literally nothing to be seen but lamps. Street after street, and all the folks asleep—street after street, all lighted up as if for a procession, and all as empty as a church—till at last I got into that state of mind when a man listens and listens and begins to long for the sight of a policeman. All at once, I saw two figures: one a little man who was stumping along eastward at a good walk, and the other a girl of maybe eight or ten who was running as hard as she was able down a cross street. Well, sir, the two ran into one another naturally enough at the corner; and then came the horrible part of the thing; for the man trampled calmly over the child's body and left her screaming on the ground. It sounds nothing to hear, but it was hellish to see. It wasn't like a man; it was like some damned Juggernaut. I gave a view halloa, took to my heels, collared my gentleman, and brought him back to where there was already quite a group about the screaming child. He was perfectly cool and made no resistance, but gave me one look, so ugly that it brought out the sweat on me like running. The people who had turned out were the girl's own family; and pretty soon the doctor, for whom she had been sent, put in his appearance. Well, the child was not much the worse, more frightened, according to the Sawbones; and there you might have supposed would be an end to it. But there was one curious circumstance. I had taken a loathing to my gentleman at first sight. So had the child's family, which was only natural. But the doctor's case was what struck me. He was the usual cut and dry apothecary, of no particular age and colour, with a strong Edinburgh accent, and about as emotional as a bagpipe. Well, sir, he was like the rest of us: every time he looked at my prisoner, I saw that Sawbones turned sick and white with the desire to kill him. I knew what was in his mind, just as he knew what was in mine; and killing being out of the question, we did the next best.

We told the man we could and would make such scandal out of this, as should make his name stink from one end of London to the other. If he had any friends or any credit, we undertook that he should lose them. And all the time, as we were pitching it in red hot, we were keeping the women off him as best we could, for they were as wild as harpies. I never saw a circle of such hateful faces; and there was the man in the middle, with a kind of black, sneering coolness—frightened too, I could see that— but carrying it off, sir, really like Satan. 'If you choose to make capital out of this accident,' said he, 'I am naturally helpless. No gentleman but wishes to avoid a scene,' says he. 'Name your figure.' Well, we screwed him up to a hundred pounds for the child's family; he would have dearly liked to stick out; but there was something about the lot of us that meant mischief, and at last he struck. The next thing was to get the money; and where do you think he carried us but to that place with the door?—whipped out a key, went in, and presently came back with the matter of ten pounds in gold and a cheque for the balance on Coutts's, drawn payable to bearer, and signed with a name that I can't mention, though it's one of the points of my story, but it was a name at least very well known and often printed. The figure was stiff; but the signature was good for more than that, if it was only genuine. I took the liberty of pointing out to my gentleman that the whole business looked apocryphal; and that a man does not, in real life, walk into a cellar door at four in the morning and come out of it with another man's cheque for close upon a hundred pounds. But he was quite easy and sneering. 'Set your mind at rest,' says he; 'I will stay with you till the banks open, and cash the cheque myself.' So we all set off, the doctor, and the child's father, and our friend and myself, and passed the rest of the night in my chambers; and next day, when we had breakfasted, went in a body to the bank. I gave in the cheque myself, and said I had every reason to believe it was a forgery. Not a bit of it. The cheque was genuine."

"Tut-tut!" said Mr Utterson.

"I see you feel as I do," said Mr Enfield. "Yes, it's a bad story. For my man was a fellow that nobody could have to do with, a really damnable man; and the person that drew the cheque is the very pink of the proprieties, celebrated too, and (what makes it worse) one of your fellows who do what they call good. Blackmail, I suppose; an honest man paying through the nose for some of the capers of his youth. Blackmail House is what I call that Place with the door, in consequence. Though even that, you know, is far from explaining all," he added, and with the words fell into a vein of musing.

From this he was recalled by Mr Utterson asking rather suddenly: "And you don't know if the drawer of the cheque lives there?"

"A likely place, isn't it?" returned Mr Enfield. "But I happen to have noticed his address; he lives in some square or other."

"And you never asked about—the place with the door?" said Mr Utterson.

"No, sir; I had a delicacy," was the reply. "I feel very strongly about putting questions; it partakes too much of the style of the day of judgment. You start a question, and it's like starting a stone. You sit quietly on the top of a hill; and away the stone goes, starting others; and presently some bland old bird (the last you would

have thought of) is knocked on the head in his own
back garden, and the family have to change their
name. No, sir, I make it a rule of mine: the more it
looks like Queer Street, the less I ask."

"A very good rule, too," said the lawyer.

"But I have studied the place for myself," continued
Mr Enfield. "It seems scarcely a house. There is no
other door, and nobody goes in or out of that one, but,
once in a great while, the gentleman of my adventure.
There are three windows looking on the court on the
first floor, none below; the windows are always shut,
but they're clean. And then there is a chimney, which
is generally smoking; so somebody must live there.
And yet it's not so sure; for the buildings are so packed
together about that court, that it's hard to say where
one ends and another begins."

The pair walked on again for a while in silence; and
then—"Enfield," said Mr Utterson, "that's a good rule
of yours."

"Yes, I think it is," returned Enfield.

"But for all that," continued the lawyer, "there's one
point I want to ask: I want to ask the name of the man
who walked over the child."

"Well," said Mr Enfield, "I can't see what harm it
would do. It was a man of the name of Hyde."

"H'm," said Mr Utterson. "What sort of a man is he
to see?"

"He is not easy to describe. There is something
wrong with his appearance; something displeasing,
something downright detestable. I never saw a man I
so disliked, and yet I scarce know why. He must be
deformed somewhere; he gives a strong feeling of deformity, although I couldn't specify the point. He's an

extraordinary-looking man, and yet I really can name nothing out of the way. No, sir; I can make no hand of it; I can't describe him. And it's not want of memory; for I declare I can see him this moment."

Mr Utterson again walked some way in silence, and obviously under a weight of consideration. "You are sure he used a key?" he inquired at last.

"My dear sir——" began Enfield, surprised out of himself.

"Yes, I know," said Utterson; "I know it must seem strange. The fact is, if I do not ask you the name of the other party, it is because I know it already. You see, Richard, your tale has gone home. If you have been inexact in any point, you had better correct it."

"I think you might have warned me," returned the other, with a touch of sullenness. "But I have been pedantically exact, as you call it. The fellow had a key; and, what's more he has it still. I saw him use it, not a week ago."

Mr Utterson sighed deeply, but said never a word; and the young man presently resumed. "Here is another lesson to say nothing," said he. "I am ashamed of my long tongue. Let us make a bargain never to refer to this again."

"With all my heart," said the lawyer. "I shake hands on that, Richard."

2

Search for Mr Hyde

That evening Mr Utterson came home to his bachelor house in sombre spirits, and sat down to dinner without relish. It was his custom of a Sunday, when this meal was over, to sit close by the fire, a volume of some dry divinity on his reading desk, until the clock of the neighbouring church rang out the hour of twelve, when he would go soberly and gratefully to bed. On this night, however, as soon as the cloth was taken away, he took up a candle and went into his business room. There he opened his safe, took from the most private part of it a document endorsed on the envelope as Dr Jekyll's Will, and sat down with a clouded brow to study its contents. The will was holograph; for Mr Utterson, though he took charge of it now that it was made, had refused to lend the least assistance in the making of it; it provided not only that, in case of the decease of Henry Jekyll, M.D., D.C.L., LL.D., F.R.S., etc., all his possessions were to pass into the hands of his "friend and benefactor Edward Hyde", but that in case of Dr Jekyll's "disappearance or unexplained absence for any period exceeding three calendar months," the said Edward Hyde should step into the said Henry Jekyll's shoes without further delay, and free from any burthen or obligation, beyond the payment of a few small sums to the members of the doctor's household. This document had long been the lawyer's eyesore. It offended him both as a lawyer and as a lover of the sane and customary sides of life, to whom the fanciful was the immodest. And hitherto it was his ignorance of Mr Hyde that had swelled his indignation; now, by a sudden turn, it was his knowledge. It was already bad enough when the name was but a name of which he could learn no more. It was worse when it began to be clothed upon with detestable attributes; and out of the shifting, insubstantial mists that had so long baffled his eye, there leaped up the sudden, definite presentment of a fiend.

"I thought it was madness," he said, as he replaced the obnoxious paper in the safe; "and now I begin to fear it is disgrace."

With that he blew out his candle, put on a greatcoat, and set forth in the direction of Cavendish Square, that citadel of medicine, where his friend, the great Dr Lanyon, had his house and received his crowding patients. "If anyone knows, it will be Lanyon," he had thought.

The solemn butler knew and welcomed him; he was subjected to no stage of delay, but ushered direct from the door to the dining-room, where Dr Lanyon sat alone over his wine. This was a hearty, healthy, dapper, red-faced gentleman, with a shock of hair prematurely white, and a boisterous and decided manner. At sight of Mr Utterson, he sprang up from his chair and welcomed him with both hands. The geniality, as was the way of the man, was somewhat theatrical to the eye, but it reposed on genuine feeling. For these two were old friends, old mates both at school and college, both thorough respecters of themselves and of each other, and, what does not always follow, men who thoroughly enjoyed each other's company.

After a little rambling talk, the lawyer led up to the subject which so disagreeably preoccupied his mind.

"I suppose, Lanyon," said he, "you and I must be the two oldest friends that Henry Jekyll has?"

"I wish the friends were younger," chuckled Dr Lanyon. "But I suppose we are. And what of that? I see little of him now."

"Indeed!" said Utterson. "I thought you had a bond of common interest."

"We had," was the reply. "But it is more than ten years since Henry Jekyll became too fanciful for me. He began to go wrong, wrong in mind; and though, of course, I continue to take an interest in him for old sake's sake as they say, I see and I have seen devilish little of the man. Such unscientific balderdash," added the doctor, flushing suddenly purple, "would have estranged Damon and Pythias."

This little spirit of temper was somewhat of a relief to Mr Utterson. "They have only differed on some point of science," he thought; and being a man of no scientific passions (except in the matter of conveyancing) he even added: "It is nothing worse than that!" He gave his friend a few seconds to recover his composure, and then approached the question he had come to put.

"Did you ever come across a protégé of his—one Hyde?" he asked.

"Hyde?" repeated Lanyon. "No. Never heard of him. Since my time."

That was the amount of information that the lawyer carried back with him to the great, dark bed on which he tossed to and fro, until the small hours of the morning began to grow large. It was a night of little ease to his toiling mind, toiling in mere darkness and besieged by questions.

Six o'clock struck on the bells of the church that was so conveniently near to Mr Utterson's dwelling, and still he was digging at the problem. Hitherto it had touched him on the intellectual side alone; but now his imagination also was engaged, or rather enslaved; and as he lay and tossed in the gross darkness of the night and the curtained room, Mr Enfield's tale went by before his mind in a scroll of lighted pictures. He would be aware of the great field of lamps of a nocturnal city; then of the figure of a man walking swiftly; then of a child running from the doctor's; and then these met, and that human Juggernaut trod the child down and passed on regardless of her screams. Or else he would see a room in a rich house, where his friend lay asleep, dreaming and smiling at his dreams; and then the door of that room would be opened, the curtains of the bed plucked apart, the sleeper recalled, and, lo! there would stand by his side a figure to whom power was given, and even at that dead hour he must rise and do its bidding. The figure in these two phases haunted the lawyer all night; and if at any time he dozed over, it was but to see it glide more stealthily through sleeping houses, or move the more swiftly and still the more swiftly, even to dizziness, through wider labyrinths of lamplighted city, and at every street corner crush a child and leave her screaming. And still the figure had no face by which he might know it; even in his dreams, it had no face, or one that baffled him and melted before his eyes; and thus it was that there sprang up and grew apace in the lawyer's mind a singularly strong, almost an inordinate, curiosity to behold the features of the real Mr Hyde. If he could but once set eyes on him, he thought the mystery would lighten and perhaps roll altogether away, as was the habit of mysterious things when well examined. He might see a reason for his friend's strange preference or bondage (call it which you please), and even for the startling clauses of the will. And at least it would be a face worth seeing; the face of a man who was without bowels of mercy; a face which had but to show itself to raise up, in the mind of the unimpressionable Enfield, a spirit of enduring hatred.

From that time forward, Mr Utterson began to haunt the door in the by-street of shops. In the morning before office hours, at noon when business was plenty and time scarce, at night under the face of the fogged city moon, by all lights and at all hours of solitude or concourse, the lawyer was to be found on his chosen post.

"If he be Mr Hyde," he had thought, "I shall be Mr Seek."

And at last his patience was rewarded. It was a fine dry night; frost in the air; the streets as clean as a ballroom floor; the lamps, unshaken by any wind, drawing a regular pattern of light and shadow. By ten o'clock, when the shops were closed, the by-street was very solitary, and, in spite of the low growl of London from all round, very silent. Small sounds carried far; domestic sounds out of the houses were dearly audible on either side of the roadway; and the rumour of the approach of any passenger preceded him by a long time.

Mr Utterson had been some minutes at his post when he was aware of an odd, light footstep drawing near. In the course of his nightly patrols he had long grown accustomed to the quaint effect with which the footfalls of a single person, while he is still a great way off, suddenly spring out distinct from the vast hum and clatter of the city. Yet his attention had never before been so sharply and decisively arrested; and it was with a strong, superstitious prevision of success that he withdrew into the entry of the court.

The steps drew swiftly nearer, and swelled out suddenly louder as they turned the end of the street. The lawyer, looking forth from the entry, could soon see what manner of man he had to deal with. He was small, and very plainly dressed; and the look of him, even at that distance, went somehow strongly against the watcher's inclination. But he made straight for the door, crossing the roadway to save time; and as he came, he drew a key from his pocket, like one approaching home.

Mr Utterson stepped out and touched him on the shoulder as he passed. "Mr Hyde, I think?"

Mr Hyde shrank back with a hissing intake of the breath. But his fear was only momentary; and though he did not look the lawyer in the face, he answered coolly enough: "That is my name. What do you want?"

"I see you are going in," returned the lawyer. "I am an old friend of Dr Jekyll's—Mr Utterson, of Gaunt Street—you must have heard my name; and meeting you so conveniently, I thought you might admit me."

"You will not find Dr Jekyll; he is from home," replied Mr Hyde, blowing in the key. And then suddenly, but still without looking up, "How did you know me?" he asked.

"On your side," said Mr Utterson, "will you do me a favour?"

"With pleasure," replied the other. "What shall it be?"

"Will you let me see your face?" asked the lawyer.

Mr Hyde appeared to hesitate; and then, as if upon some sudden reflection, fronted about with an air of defiance; and the pair stared at each other pretty fixedly for a few seconds. "Now I shall know you again," said Mr Utterson. "It may be useful."

"Yes," returned Mr Hyde, "it is as well we have met; and à propos, you should have my address." And he gave a number of a street in Soho.

"Good God!" thought Mr Utterson, "can he too have been thinking of the will?" But he kept his feelings to himself, and only grunted in acknowledgement of the address.

"And now," said the other, "how did you know me?"

"By description," was the reply.

"Whose description?"

"We have common friends," said Mr Utterson.

"Common friends!" echoed Mr Hyde, a little hoarsely. "Who are they?"

"Jekyll, for instance," said the lawyer.

"He never told you," cried Mr Hyde, with a flush of anger. "I did not think you would have lied."

The other snarled aloud into a savage laugh; and the next moment, with extraordinary quickness, he had unlocked the door and disappeared into the house.

The lawyer stood awhile when Mr Hyde had left him the picture of disquietude. Then he began slowly to mount the street, pausing every step or two, and putting his hand to his brow like a man in mental perplexity. The problem he was thus debating as he walked was one of a class that is rarely solved. Mr Hyde was pale and dwarfish; he gave an impression of deformity without any nameable malformation, he had a displeasing smile, he had borne himself to the lawyer with a sort of murderous mixture of timidity and boldness, and he spoke with a husky, whispering, and somewhat broken voice—all these were points against him; but not all of these together could explain the hitherto unknown disgust, loathing, and fear with which Mr Utterson regarded him. "There must be something else," said the perplexed gentleman. "There is something more, if I could find a name for it. God bless me, the man seems hardly human! Something troglodytic, shall we say? or can it be the old story of Dr Fell? or is it the mere radiance of a foul soul that thus transpires through, and transfigures, its clay continent? The last, I think; for oh, my poor old Harry Jekyll if ever I read Satan's signature upon a face, it is on that of your new friend."

Round the corner from the by-street there was a square of ancient, handsome houses, now for the most part decayed from their high estate, and let in flats and chambers, to all sorts and conditions of men: map-engravers, architects, shady lawyers, and the agents of obscure enterprises. One house, however, second from the corner, was still occupied entire; and at the door of this, which wore a great air of wealth and comfort, though it was now plunged in darkness except for the fanlight, Mr Utterson stopped and knocked. A well-dressed, elderly servant opened the door.

"Is Dr Jekyll at home, Poole?" asked the lawyer.

"I will see, Mr Utterson," said Poole, admitting the visitor, as he spoke, into a large, low-roofed, comfortable hall, paved with flags warmed (after the fashion of a country house) by a bright, open fire, and furnished with costly cabinets of oak. "Will you wait here by the fire, sir? or shall I give you a light in the dining-room?"

"Here, thank you," said the lawyer; and he drew near and leaned on the tall fender. This hall, in which he was now left alone was a pet fancy of his friend the doctor's; and Utterson himself was wont to speak of it as the pleasantest room in London. But tonight there was a shudder in his blood; the face of Hyde sat heavy on his memory; he felt (what was rare with him) a nausea and distaste of life; and in the gloom of his spirits, he seemed to read a menace in the flickering of the firelight on the polished cabinets and the uneasy starting of the shadow on the roof. He was ashamed of his relief when Poole presently returned to announce that Dr Jekyll was gone out.

"I saw Mr Hyde go in by the old dissecting-room door, Poole," he said. "Is that right, when Dr Jekyll is from home?"

"Quite right, Mr Utterson, sir," replied the servant. "Mr Hyde has a key."

"Your master seems to repose a great deal of trust in that young man, Poole," resumed the other, musingly.

"Yes, sir, he do indeed," said Poole. "We have all orders to obey him."

"I do not think I ever met Mr Hyde?" asked Utterson.

"O dear no, sir. He never *dines* here," replied the butler. "Indeed, we see very little of him on this side of the house; he mostly comes and goes by the laboratory."

"Well, good night, Poole."

"Good night, Mr Utterson."

And the lawyer set out homeward with a very heavy heart. "Poor Harry Jekyll," he thought, "my mind misgives me he is in deep waters ! He was wild when he was young, a long while ago, to be sure; but in the law of God, there is no statute of limitations. Ah, it must be that; the ghost of some old sin, the cancer of some concealed disgrace; punishment coming, *pede claudo,* years after memory has forgotten and self-love condoned the fault." And the lawyer, scared by the thought, brooded awhile on his own past, groping in all the corners of memory, lest by chance some Jack-in-the-Box of an old iniquity should leap to light there. His past was fairly blameless; few men could read the rolls of their life with less apprehension; yet he was humbled to the dust by the many ill things he had done, and raised up again into a sober and fearful gratitude by the many that he had come so near to doing, yet avoided. And then by a return on his former subject, he conceived a spark of hope. "This Master Hyde, if he were studied," thought he, "must have secrets of his own, black secrets, by the look of him, secrets compared to which poor Jekyll's worst would be like sunshine. Things cannot continue as they are. It turns me cold to think of this creature stealing like a thief to Harry's bedside; poor Harry, what a wakening! And the danger of it! for if this Hyde suspects the existence of the will, he may grow impatient to inherit. Ah, I must put my shoulder to the wheel—if Jekyll will but let me," he added, "if Jekyll will only let me." For once more he saw before his mind's eye, as clear as a transparency, the strange clauses of the will.

3

Dr Jekyll was Quite at Ease

A fortnight later, by excellent good fortune, the doctor gave one of his pleasant dinners to some five or six old cronies, all intelligent, reputable men, and all judges of good wine; and Mr Utterson so contrived that he remained behind after the others had departed. This was no new arrangement, but a thing that had befallen many scores of times. Where Utterson was liked, he was liked well. Hosts loved to detain the dry lawyer, when the light-hearted and the loose-tongued had already their foot on the threshold; they liked to sit awhile in his unobtrusive company, practising for solitude, sobering their minds in the man's rich silence, after the expense and strain of gaiety. To this rule Dr Jekyll was no exception; and as he now sat on the opposite side of the fire—a large, well-made, smooth-faced man of fifty, with something of a slyish cast perhaps, but every mark of capacity and kindness—you could see by his looks that he cherished for Mr Utterson a sincere and warm affection.

"I have been wanting to speak to you, Jekyll," began the latter. "You know that will of yours?"

A close observer might have gathered that the topic was distasteful; but the doctor carried it off gaily. "My poor Utterson," said he, "you are unfortunate in such a client. I never saw a man so distressed as you were by my will unless it were that hide-bound pedant, Lanyon, at what he called my scientific heresies. Oh, I know he's a good fellow—you needn't frown—an excellent fellow, and I always mean to see more of him; but a hide-bound pedant for all that, an ignorant blatant pedant. I was never more disappointed in any man than Lanyon."

"You know I never approved of it" pursued Utterson, ruthlessly disregarding the fresh topic.

"My will? Yes, certainly, I know that," said the doctor, a trifle sharply. "You have told me so."

"Well, I tell you so again," continued the lawyer. "I have been learning something of young Hyde."

The large, handsome face of Dr Jekyll grew pale to the very lips, and there came a blackness about his eyes. "I do not care to hear more," said he. "this is a matter I thought we had agreed to drop."

"What I heard was abominable," said Utterson.

"It can make no change. You do not understand my position," returned the doctor, with a certain incoherency of manner. "I am painfully situated, Utterson; my position is a very strange—a very strange one. It is one of those affairs that cannot be mended by talking."

"Jekyll," said Utterson, "you know me: I am a man to be trusted. Make a clean breast of this in confidence, and I make no doubt I can get you out of it."

"My good Utterson," said the doctor, "this is very good of you, this is downright good of you, and I cannot find words to thank you in. I believe you fully; I would trust you before any man alive, aye, before myself, if I could make the choice; but indeed it isn't what you fancy; it is not so bad as that; and just to put your good heart at rest, I will tell you one thing: the moment I choose, I can be rid of Mr Hyde. I give you my hand upon that; and I thank you again and again; I will just add one little word, Utterson, that I'm sure you'll take in good part: this is a private matter, and I beg of you to let it sleep."

Utterson reflected a little, looking in the fire.

"I have no doubt you are perfectly right," he said at last, getting to his feet.

"Well, but since we have touched upon this business, and for the last time, I hope," continued the doctor, "there is one point I should like you to understand. I have really a very great interest in poor Hyde. I know you have seen him; he told me so; and I fear he was rude. But I do sincerely take a great, a very great interest in that young man; and if I am taken away, Utterson, I wish you to promise that you will bear with him and get his rights for him. I think you would, if you knew all; and it would be a weight off my mind if you would promise."

"I can't pretend that I shall ever like him," said the lawyer.

"I don't ask that," pleaded Jekyll, laying his hand upon the other's arm; "I only ask for justice; I only ask you to help him for my sake, when I am no longer here."

Utterson heaved an irrepressible sigh. "Well," said he, "I promise."

4

The Carew Murder Case

Nearly a year later, in the month of October, 18—, London was startled by a crime of singular ferocity, and rendered all the more notable by the high position of the victim. The details were few and startling. A maidservant living alone in a house not far from the river, had gone upstairs to bed about eleven. Although a fog rolled over the city in the small hours, the early part of the night was cloudless, and the lane, which the maid's window overlooked, was brilliantly lit by the full moon. It seems she was romantically given; for she sat down upon her box, which stood immediately under the window, and fell into a dream of musing. Never (she used to say, with streaming tears, when she narrated that experience), never had she felt more at peace with all men or thought more kindly of the world. And as she so sat she became aware of an aged and beautiful gentleman with white hair, drawing near along the lane; and advancing to meet him, another and very small gentleman, to whom at first she paid less attention. When they had come within speech (which was just under the maid's eyes) the older man bowed and accosted the other with a very pretty manner of politeness. It did not seem as if the subject of his address were of great importance; indeed, from his pointing, it sometimes appeared as if he were only inquiring his way; but the moon shone on his face as he spoke, and the girl was pleased to watch it, it seemed to breathe such an innocent and old-world kindness of disposition, yet with something high too, as of a well-founded self-content. Presently her eye wandered to the other, and she was surprised to recognize in him a certain Mr Hyde, who had once visited her master, and for whom she had conceived a dislike. He had in his hand a heavy cane, with which he was trifling; but he answered never a word, and seemed to listen with an ill-contained impatience. And then all of a sudden he broke out in a great flame of anger, stamping with his foot, brandishing the cane, and carrying on (as the maid described it) like a madman. The old gentleman took a step back, with the air of one very much surprised and a trifle hurt; and at that Mr Hyde broke out of all bounds, and clubbed him to the earth. And next moment, with ape-like fury, he was trampling his victim under foot, and hailing down a storm of blows, under which the bones were audibly shattered and the body jumped upon the roadway. At the horror of these sights and sounds the maid fainted.

It was two o'clock when she came to herself and called for the police. The murderer was gone long ago; but there lay his victim in the middle of the lane, incredibly mangled. The stick with which the deed had been done, although it was of some rare and very tough and heavy wood, had broken in the middle under the stress of this insensate cruelty; and one splintered half had rolled in the neighbouring gutter—the other, without doubt, had been carried away by the murderer. A purse and a gold watch were found upon the victim; but no cards or papers, except a sealed and stamped envelope, which he had been probably carrying to the post, and which bore the name and address of Mr Utterson.

This was brought to the lawyer the next morning before he was out of bed; and he had no sooner seen it, and been told the circumstances, than he shot out a solemn lip. "I shall say nothing till I have seen the body," said he; "this may be very serious. Have the kindness to wait while I dress." And with the same grave countenance he hurried through his breakfast and drove to the police station, whither the body had been carried. As soon as he came into the cell, he nodded.

"Yes," said he, "I recognize him. I am sorry to say that this is Sir Danvers Carew."

"Good God, sir," exclaimed the officer, "is it possible?" And the next moment his eye lighted up with professional ambition. "This will make a deal of noise," he said. "And perhaps you can help us to the man." And he briefly narrated what the maid had seen, and showed the broken stick.

Mr Utterson had already quailed at the name of Hyde; but when the stick was laid before him, he could doubt no longer: broken and battered as it was, he recognized it for one that he had himself presented many years before to Henry Jekyll.

"Is this Mr Hyde a person of small stature?" he inquired.

"Particularly small and particularly wicked-looking is what the maid calls him," said the officer.

Mr Utterson reflected; and then, raising his head, "If you will come with me in my cab," he said, "I think I can take you to his house."

It was by this time about nine in the morning, and the first fog of the season. A great chocolate-coloured pall lowered over heaven, but the wind was continually charging and routing these embattled vapours, so that as the cab crawled from street to street. Mr Utterson beheld a marvellous number of degrees and hues of twilight; for here it would be dark like the back-end of evening; and there would be a glow of a rich, lurid brown, like the light of some strange conflagration; and here, for a moment, the fog would be quite broken up, and a haggard shaft of daylight would glance in between the swirling wreaths. The dismal quarter of Soho seen under these changing glimpses, with its muddy ways, and slatternly passengers, and its lamps, which had never been extinguished or had been kindled afresh to combat this mournful reinvasion of darkness, seemed, in the lawyer's eyes, like a district of some city in a nightmare. The thoughts of his mind, besides, were of the gloomiest dye; and when he glanced at the companion of his drive, he was conscious of some touch of that terror of the law and the law's officers, which may at times assail the most honest.

As the cab drew up before the address indicated, the fog lifted a little and showed him a dingy street, a gin palace, a low French eating-house, a shop for the retail of penny numbers and twopenny salads, many ragged children huddled in the doorways, and many women of many different nationalities passing out, key in hand, to have a morning glass; and the next moment the fog settled down again upon that part, as brown as umber, and cut him off from his blackguardly surroundings. This was the home of Henry Jekyll's favourite, of a man who was heir to a quarter of a million sterling.

An ivory-faced and silvery-haired old woman opened the door. She had an evil face, smoothed by hypocrisy, but her manners were excellent. Yes, she said, this was Mr Hyde's, but he was not at home; he had been in that night very late, but had gone away again in less than an hour: there was nothing strange in that; his habits were very irregular, and he was often absent; for instance, it was nearly two months since she had seen him till yesterday.

"Very well then, we wish to see his rooms," said the lawyer; and when the woman began to declare it was impossible, "I had better tell you who this person is," he added. "This is Inspector Newcomen, of Scotland Yard."

A flash of odious joy appeared upon the woman's face. "Ah!" said she, "he is in trouble! What has he done?"

Mr Utterson and the inspector exchanged glances. "He don't seem a very popular character," observed the latter. "And now, my good woman, just let me and this gentleman have a look about us."

In the whole extent of the house, which but for the old woman remained otherwise empty, Mr Hyde had only used a couple of rooms; but these were furnished with luxury and good taste. A closet was filled with wine; the plate was of silver, the napery elegant; a good picture hung upon the walls, a gift (as Utterson supposed) from Henry Jekyll, who was much of a connoisseur; and the carpets were of many piles and agreeable in colour. At this moment, however, the rooms bore every mark of having been recently and hurriedly ransacked; clothes lay about the floor, with their pockets inside out; lockfast drawers stood open;

and on the hearth there lay a pile of grey ashes, as though many papers had been burned. From these embers the inspector disinterred the butt end of a green cheque-book, which had resisted the action of the fire; the other half of the stick was found behind the door; and as this clinched his suspicions, the officer declared himself delighted. A visit to the bank, where several thousand pounds were found to be lying to the murderer's credit, completed his gratification.

"You may depend upon it, sir," he told Mr Utterson, "I have him in my hand. He must have lost his head, or he never would have left the stick or, above all, burned the cheque-book. Why, money's life to the man. We have nothing to do but wait for him at the bank, and get out the handbills."

This last, however, was not so easy of accomplishment; for Mr Hyde had numbered few familiars—even the master of the servant maid had only seen him twice; his family could nowhere be traced; he had never been photographed; and the few who could describe him differed widely, as common observers will. Only on one point were they agreed; and that was, the haunting sense of unexpressed deformity with which the fugitive impressed his beholders.

5

Incident of the Letter

It was late in the afternoon when Mr Utterson found
his way to Dr Jekyll's door, where he was at once admitted by Poole, and carried down by the kitchen offices and across a yard which had once been a garden,
to the building which was indifferently known as the
laboratory or the dissecting-rooms. The doctor had
bought the house from the heirs of a celebrated surgeon; and his own tastes being rather chemical than
anatomical, had changed the destination of the block
at the bottom of the garden. It was the first time that
the lawyer had been received in that part of his friend's
quarters; and he eyed the dingy, windowless structure
with curiosity, and gazed round with a distasteful
sense of strangeness as he crossed the theatre, once
crowded with eager students and now lying gaunt and
silent, the tables laden with chemical apparatus, the
floor strewn with crates and littered with packing
straw, and the light falling dimly through the foggy cu-
pola. At the farther end, a flight of stairs mounted to a
door covered with red baize; and through this, Mr
Utterson was at last received into the doctor's cabinet.
It was a large room, fitted round with glass presses,
furnished, among other things with a cheval-glass and
a business table, and looking out upon the court by

three dusty windows barred with iron. The fire burned in the grate; a lamp was set lighted on the chimney shelf, for even in the houses the fog began to lie thickly; and there, close up to the warmth, sat Dr Jekyll, looking deadly sick. He did not rise to meet his visitor, but held out a cold hand, and bade him welcome in a changed voice.

"And now," said Mr Utterson, as soon as Poole had left them, "you have heard the news?"

The doctor shuddered. "They were crying it in the square," he said. "I heard them in my dining-room."

"One word," said the lawyer. "Carew was my client, but so are you; and I want to know what I am doing. You have not been mad enough to hide this fellow?"

"Utterson, I swear to God," cried the doctor, "I swear to God I will never set eyes on him again. I bind my honour to you that I am done with him in this world. It is all at an end. And indeed he does not want my help; you do not know him as I do; he is safe, he is quite safe; mark my words, he will never more be heard of"

The lawyer listened gloomily; he did not like his friend's feverish manner. "You seem pretty sure of him," said he; "and, for your sake, I hope you may be right. If it came to a trial, your name might appear."

"I am quite sure of him," replied Jekyll; "I have grounds for certainty that I cannot share with anyone. But there is one thing you may advise me. I have—I have received a letter; and I am at a loss whether I should show it to the police. I should like to leave it in your hands, Utterson; you would judge wisely, I am sure; I have so great a trust in you."

"You fear, I suppose, that it might lead to his detection?" asked the lawyer.

"No," said the other. "I cannot say that I care what

becomes of Hyde; I am quite done with him. I was thinking of my own character, which this hateful business has rather exposed."

Utterson ruminated awhile; he was surprised at his friend's selfishness, and yet relieved by it. "Well." said he, at last, "let me see the letter."

The letter was written in an odd, upright hand, and signed "Edward Hyde"; and it signified, briefly enough that the writer's benefactor, Dr Jekyll, whom he had long so unworthily repaid for a thousand generosities, need labour under no alarm for his safety, as he had means of escape on which he placed a sure independence. The lawyer liked this letter well enough: it put a better colour on the intimacy than he had looked for; and he blamed himself for some of his past suspicions.

"Have you the envelope?" he asked.

"I burned it," replied Jekyll "before I thought what I was about. But it bore no postmark. The note was handed in."

"Shall I keep this and sleep upon it?" asked Utterson.

"I wish you to judge for me entirely," was the reply. "I have lost confidence in myself."

"Well, I shall consider," returned the lawyer. "And now one word more: it was Hyde who dictated the terms in your will about that disappearance?"

The doctor seemed seized with a qualm of faintness; he shut his mouth tight and nodded.

"I knew it," said Utterson. "He meant to murder you. You have had a fine escape."

"I have had what is far more to the purpose," returned the doctor solemnly: "I have had a lesson—O God, Utterson, what a lesson I have had !" And he covered his face for a moment with his hands.

On his way out, the lawyer stopped and had a word or two with Poole. "By-the-by," said he, "there was a letter handed in today: what was the messenger like?" But Poole was positive nothing had come except by post; "and only circulars by that," he added.

This news sent off the visitor with his fears renewed. Plainly the letter had come by the laboratory door; possibly, indeed, it had been written in the cabinet; and, if that were so, it must be differently judged, and handled with the more caution. The newsboys, as he went, were crying themselves hoarse along the footways: "Special edition. Shocking murder of an M.P." That was the funeral oration of one friend and client; and he could not help a certain apprehension lest the good name of another should be sucked down in the eddy of the scandal. It was, at least, a ticklish decision that he had to make; and, self-reliant as he was by habit, he began to cherish a longing for advice. It was not to be had directly; but perhaps, he thought, it might be fished for.

Presently after, he sat on one side of his own hearth, with Mr Guest, his head clerk, upon the other, and midway between, at a nicely calculated distance from the fire, a bottle of a particular old wine that had long dwelt unsunned in the foundations of his house. The fog still slept on the wing above the drowned city, where the lamps glimmered like carbuncles; and through the muffle and smother of these fallen clouds, the procession of the town's life was still rolling in through the great arteries with a sound as of a mighty wind. But the room was gay with firelight. In the bottle the acids were long ago resolved; the imperial dye had softened with time, as the colour grows richer in stained windows; and the glow of hot autumn afternoons on hillside vineyards was ready to be set free and to disperse the fogs of London. Insensibly the lawyer melted. There was no man from whom he kept fewer secrets than Mr Guest; and he was not always sure that he kept as many as he meant. Guest had often been on business to the doctor's, he knew Poole; he could scarce have failed to hear of Mr Hyde's familiarity about the house; he might draw conclusions: was it not as well, then, that he should see a letter which put that mystery to rights? and, above all, since Guest, being a great student and critic of handwriting, would consider the step natural and obliging? The clerk, besides, was a man of counsel; he would scarce read so strange a document without dropping a remark; and by that remark Mr Utterson might shape his future course.

"This is a sad business about Sir Danvers," he said.

"Yes, sir, indeed. It has elicited a great deal of public feeling," returned Guest. "The man, of course, was mad."

"I should like to hear your views on that," replied Utterson. "I have a document here in his hand-writing; it is between ourselves, for I scarce know what to do about it; it is an ugly business at the best. But there it is; quite in your way; a murderer's autograph."

Guest's eyes brightened, and he sat down at once and studied it with passion. "No, sir," he said; "not mad, but it is an odd hand."

"And by all accounts a very odd writer," added the lawyer.

Just then the servant entered with a note.

"Is that from Dr Jekyll, sir?" inquired the clerk, "I thought I knew the writing. Anything private, Mr Utterson?"

"Only an invitation to dinner. Why? do you want to see it?"

"One moment. I thank you, sir;" and the clerk laid the two sheets of paper alongside and sedulously compared their contents. "Thank you, sir," he said at last returning both; "it's a very interesting autograph."

There was a pause, during which Mr Utterson struggled with himself. "Why did you compare them, Guest ?" he inquired suddenly.

"Well, sir," returned the clerk, "there's a rather singular resemblance; the two hands are in many points identical, only differently sloped."

"Rather quaint," said Utterson.

"It is, as you say, rather quaint," returned Guest.

"I wouldn't speak of this note, you know," said the master.

"No, sir," said the clerk. "I understand."

But no sooner was Mr Utterson alone that night than he locked the note into his safe, where it reposed from that time forward. "What!" he thought. "Henry Jekyll forge for a murderer!" And his blood ran cold in his veins.

6

Remarkable Incident of Dr Lanyon

Time ran on; thousands of pounds were offered in reward, for the death of Sir Danvers was resented as a public injury; but Mr Hyde had disappeared out of the ken of the police as though he had never existed. Much of his past was unearthed, indeed, and all disreputable, tales came out of the man's cruelty, at once so callous and violent, of his vile life, of his strange associates, of the hatred that seemed to have surrounded his career; but of his present whereabouts, not a whisper. From the time he had left the house in Soho on the morning of the murder, he was simply blotted out; and gradually, as time drew on, Mr Utterson began to recover from the hotness of his alarm, and to grow more at quiet with himself. The death of Sir Danvers was, to his way of thinking, more than paid for by the disappearance of Mr Hyde. Now that that evil influence had been withdrawn, a new life began for Dr Jekyll. He came out of his seclusion, renewed relations with his friends, became once more their familiar guest and entertainer; and whilst he had always been known for charities, he was now no less distinguished for religion. He was busy, he was much in the open air, he did good; his face seemed to open and brighten, as if with an inward consciousness of service; and for more than two months, the doctor was at peace.

On the 8th of January Utterson had dined at the doctor's with a small party; Lanyon had been there; and the face of the host had looked from one to the other as in the old days when the trio were inseparable friends. On the 12th, and again on the 14th, the door was shut against the lawyer. "The doctor was confined to the house," Poole said, "and saw no one." On the 15th he tried again, and was again refused; and was again refused; and having now been used for the last two months to see his friend almost daily, he found this return of solitude to weigh upon his spirits. The fifth night, he had in Guest to dine with him; and the sixth he betook himself to Dr Lanyon's.

There at least he was not denied admittance; but when he came in, he was shocked at the change which had taken place in the doctor's appearance. He had his death-warrant written legibly upon his face. The rosy man had grown pale; his flesh had fallen away; he was visibly balder and older; and yet it was not so much these tokens of a swift physical decay that arrested the lawyer's notice, as a look in the eye and quality of manner that seemed to testify to some deep-seated terror of the mind. It was unlikely that the doctor should fear death; and yet that was what Utterson was tempted to suspect. "Yes," he thought; "he is a doctor, he must know his own state and that his days are counted; and the knowledge is more than he can bear." And yet when Utterson remarked on his ill looks, it was with an air of great firmness that Lanyon declared himself a doomed man.

"I have had a shock," he said, "and I shall never recover. It is a question of weeks. Well, life has been pleasant; I liked it; yes, sir, I used to like it. I sometimes think if we knew all, we should be more glad to get away."

"Jeckyll is ill, too," observed Utterson. "Have you seen him?"

But Lanyon's face changed, and he held up a trembling hand. "I wish to see or hear no more of Dr Jekyll," he said, in a loud, unsteady voice. "I am quite done with that person; and I beg that you will spare me any allusion to one whom I regard as dead.'

"Tut, tut!" said Mr Utterson; and then, after a considerable pause, "Can't I do anything?" he inquired. "We are three very old friends, Lanyon; we shall not live to make others."

"Nothing can be done," returned Lanyon; "ask himself."

"He will not see me," said the lawyer.

"I am not surprised at that," was the reply. "Some day, Utterson, after I am dead, you may perhaps come to learn the right and wrong of this. I cannot tell you. And in the meantime, if you can sit and talk me of other things, for God's sake, stay and do so; but if you cannot keep clear of this accursed topic, then, in God's name, go, for I cannot bear it."

As soon as he got home, Utterson sat down and wrote to Jekyll, complaining of his exclusion from the house, and asking the cause of this unhappy break with Lanyon; and the next day brought him a long answer, often very pathetically worded, and sometimes darkly mysterious in drift. The quarrel with Lanyon was incurable.

"I do not blame our old friend," Jekyll wrote, 'but I share his view that we must never meet. I mean from henceforth to lead a life of extreme seclusion; you must not be surprised, nor must you doubt my friendship, if my door is often shut even to you. You must suffer me to go my own dark way. I have brought on myself a punishment and a danger that I cannot name. If I am the chief of sinners, I am the chief of sufferers also. I could not think that this earth contained a place for sufferings and terrors so unmanning; and you can do but one thing, Utterson, to lighten this destiny, and that is, to respect my silence.' Utterson was amazed; the dark influence of Hyde had been withdrawn, the doctor had returned to his old tasks and amities; a week ago, the prospect had smiled with every promise of a cheerful and an honoured age; and now in a moment, friendship and peace of mind and the whole tenor of his life were wrecked. So great and unprepared a change pointed to madness; but in view of Lanyon's manner and words, there must lie for it some deeper ground.

A week afterwards Dr Lanyon took to his bed, and in something less than a fortnight he was dead. The night after the funeral, at which he had been sadly affected, Utterson locked the door of his business room, and sitting there by the light of a melancholy candle, drew out and set before him an envelope addressed by the hand and sealed with the seal of his dear friend. "Private: for the hands of J. G. Utterson alone, and in case of his predecease *to be destroyed unread*," so it was emphatically superscribed; and the lawyer dreaded to behold the contents. "I have buried one friend today," he thought: "what if this should cost me another?" And then he condemned the fear as a disloyalty, and broke the seal. Within there was another enclosure, likewise sealed, and marked upon the cover as "not to be opened till the death or disappearance of Dr Henry Jekyll." Utterson could not trust his eyes. Yes, it was disappearance; here again, as in the mad will, which he had long ago restored to its author, here again were the idea of a disappearance and the name of Henry Jekyll bracketed. But in the will, that idea had sprung from the sinister suggestion of the man Hyde; it was set there with a purpose all too plain and horrible. Written by the hand of Lanyon, what should it mean? A great curiosity came to the trustee, to disregard the prohibition, and dive at once to the bottom of these mysteries; but professional honour and faith to his dead friend were stringent obligations; and the packet slept in the inmost corner of his private safe.

It is one thing to mortify curiosity, another to conquer it; and it may be doubted if, from that day forth, Utterson desired the society of his surviving friend with the same eagerness. He thought of him kindly; but his thoughts were disquieted and fearful. He went to call indeed; but he was perhaps relieved to be denied admittance; perhaps, in his heart, he preferred to speak with Poole upon the doorstep, and surrounded by the air and sounds of the open city, rather than to be admitted into that house of voluntary bondage, and to sit and speak with its inscrutable recluse. Poole, had indeed, no very pleasant news to communicate. The doctor, it appeared, now more than ever confined himself to the cabinet over the laboratory, where he would sometimes even sleep: he was out of spirits, he had grown very silent, he did not read; it seemed as if he had something on his mind. Utterson became so used to the unvarying character of these reports, that he fell off little by little in the frequency of his visits.

7

Incident at the Window

It chanced on Sunday, when Mr Utterson was on his usual walk with Mr Enfield, that their way lay once again through the by-street; and that when they came in front of the door, both stopped to gaze on it.

"Well," said Enfield, "that story's at an end, at least. We shall never see more of Mr Hyde."

"I hope not," said Utterson. "Did I ever tell you that I once saw him, and shared your feeling of repulsion?"

"It was impossible to do the one without the other," returned Enfield. "And, by the way, what an ass you must have thought me, not to know that this was a back way to Dr Jekyll's! it was partly your own fault that I found it out, even when I did."

"So you found it out, did you?" said Utterson. "But if that be so, we may step into the court and take a look at the windows. To tell you the truth, I am uneasy about poor Jekyll; and even outside, I feel as if the presence of a friend might do him good."

The court was very cool and a little damp, and full of premature twilight, although the sky, high up overhead, was still bright with sunset. The middle one of the three windows was half-way open; and sitting close beside it, taking the air with an infinite sadness of mein, like some disconsolate prisoner, Utterson saw Dr Jekyll.

"What! Jekyll!" he cried. "I trust you are better."

"I am very low, Utterson," replied the doctor, drearily; "very low. It will not last long, thank God."

"You stay too much indoors," said the lawyer. "You should be out, whipping up the circulation, like Mr Enfield and me. (This is my cousin, Mr Enfield—Dr Jekyll.) Come now; get your hat, and take a quick turn with us."

"You are very good," sighed the other. "I should like to very much; but no, no, no; it is quite impossible; I dare not. But indeed, Utterson, I am very glad to see you; this is really a great pleasure. I would ask you and Mr Enfield up, but the place is really not fit."

"Why then," said the lawyer, good-naturedly, "the best thing we can do is to stay down here, and speak with you from where we are."

"That is just what I was about to venture to propose," returned the doctor, with a smile. But the words were hardly uttered, before the smile was struck out of his face and succeeded by an expression of such abject terror and despair, as froze the very blood of the two gentlemen below. They saw it but for a glimpse, for the window was instantly thrust down; but that glimpse had been sufficient, and they turned and left the court without a word. In silence, too they traversed the by-street; and it was not until they had come into a neighbouring thoroughfare, where even upon a Sunday there were still some stirrings of life, that Mr Utterson at last turned and looked at his companion. They were both pale; and there was an answering horror in their eyes.

"God forgive us! God forgive us!" said Mr Utterson.

But Mr Enfield only nodded his head very seriously, and walked on once more in silence.

8

The Last Night

Mr Utterson was sitting by his fireside one evening after dinner, when he was surprised to receive a visit from Poole.

"Bless me, Poole, what brings you here?" he cried; and then, taking a second look at him, "What ails you?" he added; "is the doctor ill?"

"Mr Utterson," said the man, "there is something wrong."

"Take a seat, and here is a glass of wine for you," said the lawyer. "Now, take your time, and tell me plainly what you want."

"You know the doctor's ways, sir," replied Poole, "and how he shuts himself up. Well, he's shut up again in the cabinet; and I don't like it, sir—I wish I may die if I like it. Mr Utterson, sir, I'm afraid."

"Now, my good man," said the lawyer, "be explicit. What are you afraid of?"

"I've been afraid for about a week," returned Poole, doggedly disregarding the question; "and I can bear it no more."

The man's appearance amply bore out his words; his manner was altered for the worse: and except for the moment when he had first announced his terror, he had not once looked the lawyer in the face. Even now, he sat with the glass of wine untasted on his knee, and his eyes directed to a corner of the floor. "I can bear it no more," he repeated.

"Come," said the lawyer, "I see you have some good reason, Poole; I see there is something seriously amiss. Try to tell me what it is."

"I think there's been foul play," said Poole hoarsely.

"Foul play!" cried the lawyer, a good deal frightened, and rather inclined to be irritated in consequence. "What foul play? What does the man mean?"

"I daren't say, sir," was the answer; "but will you, come along with me and see for yourself?"

Mr Utterson's only answer was to rise and get his hat and greatcoat; but he observed with wonder the greatness of the relief that appeared upon the butler's face, and perhaps with no less, that the wine was still untasted when he set it down to follow.

It was a wild, cold seasonable night of March, with a pale moon, lying on her back as though the wind had tilted her, and a flying wrack of the most diaphanous and lawny texture. The wind made talking difficult, and flecked the blood into the face. It seemed to have swept the streets unusually bare of passengers, besides; for Mr Utterson thought he had never seen that part of London so deserted. He could have wished it otherwise; never in his life had he been conscious of so sharp a wish to see and touch his fellow creatures; for, struggle as he might, there was borne in upon his mind a crushing anticipation of calamity. The square, when they got there, was all full of wind and dust, and the thin trees in the garden were lashing themselves along the railing Poole, who had kept all the way a pace or two ahead, now pulled up in the middle of the pavement, and in spite of the biting weather, took off his hat and mopped his brow with a red pocket-handkerchief. But for all the hurry of his coming, these were not the dews of exertion that he wiped away, but the moisture of some strangling anguish; for his face was white, and his voice, when he spoke, harsh and broken.

"Well, sir," he said, "here we are, and God grant there be nothing wrong."

"Amen, Poole," said the lawyer.

Thereupon the servant knocked in a very guarded manner; the door was opened on the chain; and a voice asked from within, "Is that you, Poole?"

"It's all right," said Poole. "Open the door."

The hall, when they entered it, was brightly lighted up; the fire was built high; and about the hearth the whole of the servants, men and women, stood huddled together like a flock of sheep. At the sight of Mr Utterson, the housemaid broke into hysterical whimpering; and the cook, crying out, "Bless God! it's Mr Utterson," ran forward as if to take him in her arms.

"What, what! Are you all here?" said the lawyer, peevishly. "Very irregular, very unseemly; your master would be far from pleased."

"They're all afraid," said Poole.

Blank silence followed, no one protesting; only the maid lifted up her voice, and now wept loudly.

"Hold your tongue!" Poole said to her, with a ferocity of accent that testified to his own jangled nerves; and indeed when the girl had so suddenly raised the note of her lamentation, they had all started and turned towards the inner door with faces of dreadful expectation. "And now," continued the butler, addressing the knife boy, "reach me a candle, and we'll get this through hands at once." And then he begged Mr Utterson to follow him, and led the way to the back garden.

"Now, sir," said he, "you come as gently as you can. I want you to hear, and I don't want you to be heard. And see here, sir, if by any chance he was to ask you in, don't go."

Mr Utterson's nerves, at this unlooked-for termination, gave a jerk that nearly threw him from his balance; but he recollected his courage, and followed the butler into the laboratory building and through the surgical theatre, with its lumber of crates and bottles, to the foot of the stair. Here Poole motioned him to stand on one side and listen; while he himself, setting down the candle and making a great and obvious call on his resolution, mounted the steps, and knocked with a somewhat uncertain hand on the red baize of the cabinet door.

"Mr Utterson, sir, asking to see you," he called; and even as he did so, once more violently signed to the lawyer to give ear.

A voice answered from within: "Tell him I cannot see anyone," it said, complainingly.

"Thank you, sir," said Poole, with a note of something like triumph in his voice; and taking up his candle, he led Mr Utterson back across the yard and into the great kitchen, where the fire was out and the beetles were leaping on the floor.

"Sir," he said, looking Mr Utterson in the eyes, "was that my master's voice?"

"It seems much changed," replied the lawyer, very pale, but giving look for look.

"Changed? Well, yes, I think so," said the butler "Have I been twenty years in this man's house to be deceived about his voice? No, sir; master's made away with; he was made away with eight days ago, when we heard him cry out upon the name of God; and *who's* in there instead of him, and why it stays there, is a thing that cries to Heaven, Mr Utterson!"

"This is a very strange tale, Poole; this is rather a wild tale, my man," said Mr Utterson, biting his finger. "Suppose it were as you suppose, supposing Dr Jekyll to have been—well, murdered, what could induce the murderer to stay? That won't hold water; it doesn't commend itself to reason."

"Well, Mr Utterson, you are a hard man to satisfy, but I'll do it yet," said Poole. "All this last week (you must know) him, or it, or whatever it is that lives in that cabinet, has been crying night and day for some sort of medicine and cannot get it to his mind. It was sometimes his way—the master's, that is—to write his orders on a sheet of paper and throw it on the stair. We've had nothing else this week back; nothing but papers, and a closed door, and the very meals left there to be smuggled in when nobody was looking. Well, sir, every day, aye, and twice and thrice in the same day there have been orders and complaints, and I have been sent flying to all the wholesale chemists in town. Every time I brought the stuff back, there would be another paper telling me to return it, because it was not pure, and another order to a different firm. This drug is wanted bitter bad, sir, whatever for."

"Have you any of these papers?" asked Mr Utterson.

Poole felt in his pocket and handed out a crumpled note, which the lawyer, bending nearer to the candle, carefully examined. Its contents ran thus: "Dr Jekyll presents his compliments to Messrs Maw. He assures them that their last sample is impure and quite useless for his present purpose. In the year 18—, Dr J. purchased a somewhat large quantity from Messrs M. He now begs them to search with the most sedulous care, and should any of the same quality be left, to forward it to him at once. Expense is no consideration. The importance of this to Dr J. can hardly be exaggerated." So far the letter had run composedly enough; but here, with a sudden splutter of the pen, the writer's emotion had broken loose. "For God's sake," he had added, "find me some of the old."

"This is a strange note," said Mr Utterson; and then, sharply, "How do you come to have it open?"

"The man at Maw's was main angry, sir, and he threw it back to me like so much dirt," returned Poole.

"This is unquestionably the doctor's hand, do you know?" resumed the lawyer.

"I thought it looked like it," said the servant, rather sulkily; and then, with another voice, "But what matters hand of write?" he said. "I've seen him!"

"Seen him?" repeated Mr Utterson. "Well?"

"That's it!" said Poole. "It was this way. I came suddenly into the theatre from the garden. It seems he had slipped out to look for this drug, or whatever it is; for the cabinet door was open, and there he was at the far end of the room, digging among the crates. He looked up when I came in, gave a kind of cry, and whipped upstairs into the cabinet. It was but for one minute that I saw him, but the hair stood upon my head like quills. Sir, if that was my master, why had he a mask upon his face? If it was my master, why did he cry out like a rat, and run from me? I have served him long enough. And then—" the man paused and passed his hand over his face.

"These are all very strange circumstances," said Mr Utterson, "but I think I begin to see daylight. Your master, Poole, is plainly seized with one of those maladies that both torture and deform the sufferer; hence, for aught I know, the alteration of his voice; hence the mask and his avoidance of his friends; hence his eagerness to find this drug, by means of which the poor soul retains some hope of ultimate recovery—God grant that he be not deceived! There is my explanation; it is sad enough, Poole, aye, and appalling to consider; but it is plain and natural, hangs well together, and delivers us from all exorbitant alarms."

"Sir," said the butler, turning to a sort of mottled pallor, "that thing was not my master, and there's the truth. My master—" here he looked round him, and began to whisper— "is a tall, fine build of a man, and this was more of a dwarf." Utterson attempted to protest. "Oh, sir," cried Poole, "do you think I do not know my master after twenty years? Do you think I do not know where his head comes to in the cabinet door, where I saw him every morning of my life? No, sir, that thing in the mask was never Dr Jekyll—God knows what it was, but it was never Dr Jekyll; and it is the belief of my heart that there was murder done."

"Poole," replied the lawyer, "if you say that, it will become my duty to make certain. Much as I desire to spare your master's feelings, much as I am puzzled about his note, which seems to prove him to be still alive, I shall consider it my duty to break in that door."

"Ah, Mr Utterson, that's talking!" cried the butler.

"And now comes the second question," resumed Utterson: "Who is going to do it?"

"Why, you and me, sir," was the undaunted reply.

"That is very well said," returned the lawyer; "and whatever comes of it, I shall make it my business to see you are no loser."

"There is an axe in the theatre," continued Poole; "and you might take the kitchen poker for yourself."

The lawyer took that rude but weighty instrument into his hand, and balanced it. "Do you know, Poole," he said, looking up, "that you and I are about to place ourselves in a position of some peril?"

"You may say so, sir, indeed," returned the butler.

"It is well, then, that we should be frank," said the other. "We both think more than we have said; let us make a clean breast. This masked figure that you saw, did you recognize it?"

"Well, sir, it went so quick, and the creature was so doubled up, that I could hardly swear to that," was the answer. "But if you mean was it Mr Hyde?—why, yes, I think it was! You see, it was much of the same bigness; and it had the same quick light way with it; and then who else could have got in by the laboratory door? You have not forgot, sir, that at the time of the murder he had still the key with him? But that's not all. I don't know, Mr Utterson, if ever you met this Mr Hyde?"

"Yes," said the lawyer, "I once spoke with him."

"Then you must know, as well as the rest of us, that there was something queer about that gentleman— something that gave a man a turn—I don't know rightly how to say it, sir, beyond this: that you felt it in your marrow—kind of cold and thin."

"I own I felt something of what you describe," said Mr Utterson.

"Quite so, sir," returned Poole. "Well, when that

masked thing like a monkey jumped from among the chemicals and whipped into the cabinet, it went down my spine like ice. Oh, I know it's not evidence, Mr Utterson; I'm book-learned enough for that; but a man has his feelings; and I give you my Bible-word it was Mr Hyde!"

"Aye, aye," said the lawyer. "My fears incline to the same point. Evil, I fear, founded—evil was sure to come—of that connection. Aye, truly, I believe you; I believe poor Harry is killed; and I believe his murderer (for what purpose, God alone can tell) is still lurking in his victim's room. Well, let our name be vengeance. Call Bradshaw."

The footman came at the summons, very white and nervous.

"Pull yourself together, Bradshaw," said the lawyer. "This suspense, I know, is telling upon all of you; but it is now our intention to make an end of it. Poole, here, and I are going to force our way into the cabinet. If all is well, my shoulders are broad enough to bear the blame. Meanwhile, lest anything should really be amiss, or any malefactor seek to escape by the back, you and the boy must go round the corner with a pair of good sticks, and take your post at the laboratory door. We give you ten minutes to get to your stations."

As Bradshaw left, the lawyer looked at his watch. "And now, Poole, let us get to ours," he said; and taking the poker under his arm, he led the way into the yard. The scud had banked over the moon, and it was now quite dark. The wind, which only broke in puffs and draughts into that deep well of buildings, tossed the light of the candle to and fro about their steps, until they came into the shelter of the theatre, where they sat down silently to wait. London hummed solemnly all around; but nearer at hand, the stillness was only broken by the sound of a footfall moving to and fro along the cabinet floor.

"So it will walk all day, sir," whispered Poole; "aye, and the better part of the night. Only when a new sample comes from the chemist, there's a bit of a break. Ah, it's an ill conscience that's such an enemy to rest! Ah, sir, there's blood foully shed in every step of it! But hark again, a little closer put your heart in your ears, Mr Utterson, and tell me, is that the doctor's foot?"

The steps fell lightly and oddly, with a certain swing, for all they went so slowly; it was different indeed from the heavy creaking tread of Henry Jekyll. Utterson sighed. "Is there never anything else?" he asked.

Poole nodded. "Once," he said. "Once I heard it weeping!"

"Weeping? how that?" said the lawyer, conscious of a sudden chill of horror.

"Weeping like a woman or a lost soul," said the butler. "I came away with that upon my heart, that I could have wept too."

But now the ten minutes drew to an end. Poole disinterred the axe from under a stack of packing straw; the candle was set upon the nearest table to light them to the attack; and they drew near with bated breath to where that patient foot was still going up and down, up and down in the quiet of the night.

"Jekyll," cried Utterson, with a loud voice, "I demand to see you." He paused a moment, but there came no reply. "I give you fair warning, our suspicions

are aroused, and I must and shall see you," he resumed; "if not by fair means, then by foul—if not of
your consent, then by brute force!"

"Utterson," said the voice, "for God's sake, have
mercy!"

"Ah, that's not Jekyll's voice—it's Hyde's!" cried
Utterson. "Down with the door, Poole!"

Poole swung the axe over his shoulder; the blow
shook the building, and the red baize door leaped
against the lock and hinges. A dismal screech, as of
mere animal terror, rang from the cabinet. Up went the
axe again, and again the panels crashed and the frame
bounded; four times the blow fell; but the wood was
tough and the fittings were of excellent workmanship;
and it was not until the fifth that the lock burst in sun-
der, and the wreck of the door fell inwards on the carpet.

The besiegers, appalled by their own riot and the
stillness that had succeeded, stood back a little and
peered in. There lay the cabinet before their eyes in the
quiet lamplight, a good fire glowing and chattering on
the hearth, the kettle singing its thin strain, a drawer or
two open, papers neatly set forth on the business table,
and nearer the fire, the things laid out for tea: the quiet-
est room, you would have said, and, but for the glazed
presses full of chemicals, the most commonplace that
night in London.

Right in the midst there lay the body of a man sorely
contorted and still twitching. They drew near on tiptoe,
turned it on its back, and beheld the face of Edward
Hyde. He was dressed in clothes far too large for him,
clothes of the doctor's bigness; the cords of his face
still moved with a semblance of life, but life was quite

gone; and by the crushed phial in the hand and the strong smell of kernels that hung upon the air, Utterson knew that he was looking on the body of a self-destroyer.

"We have come too late," he said sternly, "whether to save or punish. Hyde is gone to his account; and it only remains for us to find the body of your master."

The far greater proportion of the building was occupied by the theatre, which filled almost the whole ground story, and was lighted from above, and by the cabinet, which formed an upper story at one end and looked upon the court. A corridor joined the theatre to the door on the by-street; and with this, the cabinet communicated separately by a second flight of stairs. There were besides a few dark closets and a spacious cellar. All these they now thoroughly examined. Each closet needed but a glance, for all were empty, and all, by the dust that fell from their doors, had stood long unopened. The cellar, indeed, was filled with crazy lumber, mostly dating from the times of the surgeon who was Jekyll's predecessor; but even as they opened the door, they were advertised of the uselessness of further search, by the fall of a perfect mat of cobweb which had for years sealed up the entrance. Nowhere was there any trace of Henry Jekyll, dead or alive.

Poole stamped on the flags of the corridor. "He must be buried here," he said, hearkening to the sound.

"Or he may have fled," said Utterson, and he turned to examine the door in the by-street. It was locked; and lying near by on the flags, they found the key, already stained with rust.

"This does not look like use," observed the lawyer.

"Use!" echoed Poole. "Do you not see, sir, it is broken? much as if a man had stamped on it."

"Ah," continued Utterson, "and the fractures, too, are rusty." The two men looked at each other with a scare. "This is beyond me, Poole," said the lawyer. "Let us go back to the cabinet."

They mounted the stair in silence, and still, with an occasional awe-struck glance at the dead body, proceeded more thoroughly to examine the contents of the cabinet. At one table, there were traces of chemical work, various measured heaps of some white salt being laid on glass saucers, as though for an experiment in which the unhappy man had been prevented.

"That is the same drug that I was always bringing him," said Poole; and even as he spoke, the kettle with a startling noise boiled over.

This brought them to the fireside, where the easy chair was drawn cosily up, and the tea things stood ready to the sitter's elbow, the very sugar in the cup. There were several books on a shelf; one lay beside the tea things open, and Utterson was amazed to find it a copy of a pious work, for which Jekyll had several times expressed a great esteem, annotated, in his own hand, with startling blasphemies.

Next, in the course of their review of the chamber, the searchers came to the cheval-glass, into whose depth they looked with an involuntary horror. But it was so turned as to show them nothing but the rosy glow playing on the roof, the fire sparkling in a hundred repetitions along the glazed front of the presses, and their own pale and fearful countenances stooping to look in.

"This glass has seen some strange things, sir," whispered Poole.

"And surely none stranger than itself," echoed the lawyer, in the same tone. "For what did Jekyll"—he caught himself up at the word with a start, and then conquering the weakness: "what could Jekyll want with it?" he said.

"You may say that!" said Poole.

Next they turned to the business table. On the desk among the neat array of papers, a large envelope was uppermost, and bore, in the doctor's hand, the name of Mr Utterson. The lawyer unsealed it, and several enclosures fell to the floor. The first was a will, drawn in the same eccentric terms as the one which he had returned six months before, to serve as a testament in case of death and as a deed of gift in case of disappearance; but in place of the name of Edward Hyde, the lawyer, with indescribable amazement, read the name of Gabriel John Utterson. He looked at Poole, and then back at the papers, and last of all at the dead malefactor stretched upon the carpet.

"My head goes round," he said. He has been all these days in possession; he had no cause to like me; he must have raged to see himself displaced; and he has not destroyed this document."

He caught the next paper; it was a brief note in the doctor's hand, and dated at the top. "O Poole!" the lawyer cried, he was alive and here this day. He cannot have been disposed of in so short a space; he must be still alive, he must have fled! And then, why fled? and how? and in that case can we venture to declare this suicide? Oh, we must be careful. I foresee that we may yet involve your master in some dire catastrophe."

"Why don't you read it, sir?" asked Poole.

"Because I fear," replied the lawyer solemnly. "God

grant I have no cause for it!" And with that he brought the paper to his eye, and read as follows:

"My Dear Utterson—When this shall fall into your hands, I shall have disappeared, under what circumstances I have not the penetration to foresee; but my instincts and all the circumstances of my nameless situation tell me that the end is sure and must be early. Go then, and first read the narrative which Lanyon warned me he was to place in your hands; and if you care to hear more, turn to the confession of:

"Your unworthy and unhappy friend,

Henry Jekyll."

"There was a third enclosure?" asked Utterson.

"Here, sir," said Poole, and gave into his hands a considerable packet sealed in several places.

The lawyer put it in his pocket. "I would say nothing of this paper. If your master has fled or is dead, we may at least save his credit. It is now ten; I must go home and read these documents in quiet; but I shall be back before midnight, when we shall send for the police."

They went out, locking the door of the theatre behind them; and Utterson, once more leaving the servants gathered about the fire in the hall, trudged back to his office to read the two narratives in which this mystery was now to be explained.

9

Dr Lanyon's Narrative

On the ninth of January, now four days ago, I received
by the evening delivery a registered envelope, addressed in the hand of my colleague and old school
companion, Henry Jekyll. I was a good deal surprised
by this; for we were by no means in the habit of corre-
spondence; I had seen the man, dined with him, indeed, the night before; and I could imagine nothing in
our intercourse that should justify the formality of reg-
istration. The contents increased my wonder; for this is
how the letter ran:

10*th December* 18—.

"DEAR LANYON—You are one of my oldest friends;
and although we may have differed at times on scientific questions, I cannot remember, at least on my side,
any break in our affection. There was never a day
when, if you had said to me, 'Jekyll, my life, my honour, my reason, depend upon you,' I would not have
sacrificed my fortune or my left hand to help you.
Lanyon, my life, my honour, my reason, are all at your
mercy; if you fail me tonight, I am lost. You might suppose, after this preface, that I am going to ask you for
something dishonourable to grant. Judge for yourself.

I want you to postpone all other engagements for to-night—aye, even if you were summoned to the bed-side of an emperor; to take a cab, unless your carriage should be actually at the door; and, with this letter in your hand for consultation, to drive straight to my house. Poole, my butler, has his orders; you will find him waiting your arrival with a locksmith. The door of my cabinet is then to be forced; and you are to go in alone; to open the glazed press (letter E) on the left hand, breaking the lock if it be shut; and to draw out, *with all its contents as they stand,* the fourth drawer from the top or (which is the same thing) the third from the bottom. In my extreme distress of mind, I have a morbid fear of misdirecting you; but even if I am in error, you may know the right drawer by its con-tents: some powders, a phial, and a paper book. This drawer I beg of you to carry back with you to Cavendish Square exactly as it stands.

That is the first part of the service: now for the sec-ond. You should be back, if you set out at once on the receipt of this, long before midnight; but I will leave you that amount of margin, not only in the fear of one of those obstacles that can neither be prevented nor foreseen, but because an hour when your servants are in bed is to be preferred for what will then remain to do. At midnight, then, I have to ask you to be alone in your consulting room, to admit with your own hand into the house a man who will present himself in my name, and to place in his hands the drawer that you will have brought with you from my cabinet. Then you will have played your part, and earned my gratitude completely. Five minutes afterwards, if you insist upon an explanation, you will have understood that these arrangements are of capital importance; and that by the neglect of one of them, fantastic as they must appear, you might have charged your conscience with my death or the shipwreck of my reason.

Confident as I am that you will not trifle with this appeal, my heart sinks and my hand trembles at the bare thought of such a possibility. Think of me at this hour, in a strange place, labouring under a blackness of distress that no fancy can exaggerate, and yet well aware that, if you will but punctually serve me, my troubles will roll away like a story that is told. Serve me, my dear Lanyon, and save

Your friend,

HJ.

P.S.—I had already sealed this up when a fresh terror struck upon my soul. It is possible that the post office may fail me, and this letter not come into your hands until tomorrow morning. In that case, dear Lanyon, do my errand when it shall be most convenient for you in the course of the day; and once more expect my messenger at midnight. It may then already be too late; and if that night passes without event, you will know that you have seen the last of Henry Jekyll."

Upon the reading of this letter, I made sure my colleague was insane; but till that was proved beyond the possibility of doubt, I felt bound to do as he requested. The less I understood of this farrago, the less I was in a position to judge of its importance; and an appeal so worded could not be set aside with a grave responsibility. I rose accordingly from table, got into a hansom, and drove straight to Jekyll's house. The butler was awaiting my arrival; he had received by the same post as mine a registered letter of instruction, and had sent at once for a locksmith and a carpenter. The tradesmen came while we were yet speaking; and we moved in a body to old Dr Denman's surgical theatre, from which (as you are doubtless aware) Jekyll's private cabinet is most conveniently entered. The door was very strong, the lock excellent; the carpenter avowed he would have great trouble, and have to do much damage if force were to be used; and the locksmith was near despair. But this last was a handy fellow, and after two hours' work, the door stood open. The press marked E was unlocked; and I took out the drawer, had it filled up with straw and tied in a sheet, and returned with it to Cavendish Square.

Here I proceeded to examine its contents. The powders were neatly enough made up, but not with the nicety of the dispensing chemist; so that it was plain they were of Jekyll's private manufacture; and when I opened one of the wrappers, I found what seemed to me a simple crystalline salt of a white colour. The phial, to which I next turned my attention, might have been about half full of a blood-red liquor, which was highly pungent to the sense of smell, and seemed to me to contain phosphorus and some volatile ether. At the other ingredients I could make no guess. The book was an ordinary version book, and contained little but a series of dates. These covered a period of many years; but I observed that the entries ceased nearly a year ago, and quite abruptly. Here and there a brief remark was appended to a date, usually no more than a single word: "double" occurring perhaps six times in a total of several hundred entries; and once very early in the list, and followed by several marks of exclamation, "total failure!!!" All this, though it whetted my curiosity, told me little that was definite. Here were a phial of some tincture, a paper of some salt, and the record of a series of experiments that had led (like too many of Jekyll's investigations) to no end of practical usefulness. How could the presence of these articles in my house affect either the honour, the sanity, or the life of my flighty colleague? If his messenger could go to one place, why could he not go to another? And even granting some impediment, why was this gentleman to be received by me in secret? The more I reflected, the more convinced I grew that I was dealing with a case of cerebral disease; and though I dismissed my servants to bed, I loaded an old revolver, that I might be found in some posture of self-defence.

Twelve o'clock had scarce rung out over London, ere the knocker sounded very gently on the door. I went myself at the summons, and found a small man crouching against the pillars of the portico.

"Are you come from Dr Jekyll?" I asked.

He told me "yes" by a constrained gesture; and when I had bidden him enter, he did not obey me without a searching backward glance into the darkness of the square. There was a policeman not far off, advancing with his bull's eye open; and at the sight, I thought my visitor started and made greater haste.

These particulars struck me, I confess, disagreeably; and as I followed him into the bright light of the consulting room, I kept my hand ready on my weapon. Here, at last, I had a chance of clearly seeing him. I had never set eyes on him before, so much was certain. He was small, as I have said; I was struck besides with the shocking expression of his face, with his remarkable combination of great muscular activity and great apparent debility of constitution, and—last but not least—with the odd, subjective disturbance caused by his neighbourhood. This bore some resemblance to incipient rigor, and was accompanied by a marked sinking of the pulse. At the time, I set it down to some idiosyncratic, personal distaste, and merely wondered at the acuteness of the symptoms; but I have since had reason to believe the cause to lie much deeper in the nature of man, and to turn on some nobler hinge than the principle of hatred.

This person (who had thus, from the first moment of his entrance, struck in me what I can only describe as a disgustful curiosity) was dressed in a fashion that would have made an ordinary person laughable; his clothes, that is to say, although they were of rich and sober fabric, were enormously too large for him in every measurement—the trousers hanging on his legs and rolled up to keep them from the ground, the waist of the coat below his haunches, and the collar sprawling wide upon his shoulders. Strange to relate, this ludicrous accoutrement was far from moving me to laughter. Rather, as there was something abnormal and misbegotten in the very essence of the creature that now faced me—something seizing, surprising, and revolting—this fresh disparity seemed but to fit in with and to reinforce it; so that to my interest in the man's nature and character, there was added a curiosity as to his origin, his life, his fortune, and status in the world.

These observations, though they have taken so great a space to be set down in, were yet the work of a few seconds. My visitor was, indeed, on fire with sombre excitement.

"Have you got it?" he cried. "Have you got it?" And so lively was his impatience that he even laid his hand upon my arm and sought to shake me.

I put him back, conscious at his touch of a certain icy pang along my blood. "Come, sir," said I. "You forget that I have not yet the pleasure of your acquaintance. Be seated, if you please." And I showed him an example, and sat down myself in my customary seat and with as fair an imitation of my ordinary manner to a patient, as the lateness of the hour, the nature of my preoccupations, and the horror I had of my visitor, would suffer me to muster.

"I beg your pardon, Dr Lanyon," he replied, civilly enough: "What you say is very well founded; and my impatience has shown its heels to my politeness. I come here at the instance of your colleague, Dr Henry Jekyll, on a piece of business of some moment; and I understood—" he paused and put his hand to his throat, and I could see, in spite of his collected manner, that he was wrestling against the approaches of the hysteria— "I understood, a drawer—"

But here I took pity on my visitor's suspense, and some perhaps on my own growing curiosity.

"There it is, sir," said I, pointing to the drawer, where it lay on the floor behind a table, and still covered with the sheet.

He sprang to it, and then paused, and laid his hand upon his heart; I could hear his teeth grate with the convulsive action of his jaws; and his face was so ghastly to see that I grew alarmed both for his life and reason.

"Compose yourself," said I.

He turned a dreadful smile to me, and, as if with the

decision of despair, plucked away the sheet. At sight of
the contents, he uttered one loud sob of such immense
relief that I sat petrified. And the next moment, in a
voice that was already fairly well under control, "Have
you a graduated glass?" he asked.

I rose from my place with something of an effort,
and gave him what he asked.

He thanked me with a smiling nod, measured out a
few minims of the red tincture and added one of the
powders. The mixture, which was at first of a reddish
hue, began, in proportion as the crystals melted, to
brighten in colour, to effervesce audibly, and to throw
off small fumes of vapour. Suddenly, and at the same
moment, the ebullition ceased, and the compound
changed to a dark purple, which faded again more
slowly to a watery green. My visitor, who had watched
these metamorphoses with a keen eye, smiled, set
down the glass upon the table, and then turned and
looked upon me with an air of scrutiny.

"And now," said he, "to settle what remains. Will
you be wise? will you be guided? will you suffer me to
take this glass in my hand, and to go forth from your
house without further parley? or has the greed of curiosity too much command of you? Think before you
answer, for it shall be done as you decide. As you decide, you shall be left as you were before, and neither
richer nor wiser, unless the sense of service rendered
to a man in mortal distress may be counted as a kind of
riches of the soul. Or, if you shall so prefer to choose, a
new province of knowledge and new avenues to fame
and power shall be laid open to you, here, in this room,
upon the instant; and your sight shall be blasted by a
prodigy to stagger the unbelief of Satan."

"Sir," said I affecting a coolness that I was far from truly possessing, "you speak enigmas, and you will perhaps not wonder that I hear you with no very strong impression of belief. But I have gone too far in the way of inexplicable services to pause before I see the end."

"It is well," replied my visitor. "Lanyon, you remember your vows: what follows is under the seal of our profession. And now, you who have so long been bound to the most narrow and material views, you who have denied the virtue of transcendental medicine, you who have derided your superiors—behold!"

He put the glass to his lips, and drank at one gulp. A cry followed; he reeled, staggered, clutched at the table and held on, staring with injected eyes, gasping with open mouth; and as I looked, there came, I thought, a change—he seemed to swell—his face became suddenly black, and the features seemed to melt and alter—and the next moment I had sprung to my feet and leaped back against the wall, my arm raised to shield me from that prodigy, my mind submerged in terror.

"O God!" I screamed, and "O God!" again and again; for there before my eyes—pale and shaken, and half fainting, and groping before him with his hands, like a man restored from death—there stood Henry Jekyll!

What he told me in the next hour I cannot bring my mind to set on paper. I saw what I saw, I heard what I heard, and my soul sickened at it; and yet, now when that sight has faded from my eyes I ask myself if I believe it, and I cannot answer. My life is shaken to its roots; sleep has left me; the deadliest terror sits by me at all hours of the day and night; I feel that my days are numbered, and that I must die; and yet I shall die incredulous. As for the moral turpitude that man unveiled to me, even with tears of penitence, I cannot, even in memory, dwell on it without a start of horror. I will say but one thing, Utterson, and that (if you can bring your mind to credit it) will be more than enough. The creature who crept into my house that night was, on Jekyll's own confession, known by the name of Hyde, and hunted for in every corner of the land as the murderer of Carew.

HASTIE LANYON

10

Henry Jekyll's Full Statement of the Case

I was born in the year 18— to a large fortune, endowed besides with excellent parts, inclined by nature to industry, fond of the respect of the wise and good among my fellow men, and thus, as might have been supposed, with every guarantee of an honourable and distinguished future. And, indeed, the worst of my faults was a certain impatient gaiety of disposition, such as has made the happiness of many, but such as I found it hard to reconcile with my imperious desire to carry my head high, and wear a more than commonly grave countenance before the public. Hence it came about that I concealed my pleasures; and that when I reached years of reflection, and began to look round me, and take stock of my progress and position in the world, I stood already committed to a profound duplicity of life. Many a man would have even blazoned such irregularities as I was guilty of; but from the high views that I had set before me, I regarded and hid them with an almost morbid sense of shame. It was thus rather the exacting nature of my aspirations, than any particular degradation in my faults, that made me what I was, and, with even a deeper trench than in the majority of men, severed in me those provinces of good and ill which divide and compound man's dual nature. In this case, I was driven to reflect deeply and inveterately on that hard law of life, which lies at the root of religion, and is one of the most plentiful springs of distress. Though so profound a double-dealer, I was in no sense a hypocrite; both sides of me were in dead earnest; I was no more myself when I laid aside restraint and plunged in shame, than when I laboured, in the eye of day, at the furtherance of knowledge or the relief of sorrow and suffering. And it chanced that the direction of my scientific studies, which led wholly towards the mystic and the transcendental, reacted and shed a strong light on this consciousness of the perennial war among my members. With every day, and from both sides of my intelligence, the moral and the intellectual, I thus drew steadily nearer to that truth, by whose partial discovery I have been doomed to such a dreadful shipwreck: that man is not truly one, but truly two. I say two, because the state of my own knowledge does not pass beyond that point. Others will follow, others will outstrip me on the same lines; and I hazard the guess that man will be ultimately known for a mere polity of multifarious, incongruous, and independent denizens. I, for my part, from the nature of my life, advanced infallibly in one direction, and in one direction only. It was on the moral side, and in my own person, that I learned to recognize the thorough and primitive duality of man; I saw that, of the two natures that contended in the field of my consciousness, even if I could rightly be said to be either, it was only because I was radically both; and from an early date, even before the course of my scientific discoveries had begun to suggest the most naked possibility of such a miracle, I had learned to dwell with pleasure, as a beloved daydream, on the thought of the separation of these elements. If each, I told myself, could but be housed in separate identities, life would be relieved of all that was unbearable; the unjust might go his way, delivered from the aspirations and remorse of his more upright twin; and the just could walk steadfastly and securely on his upward path, doing the good things in which he found his pleasure, and no longer exposed to disgrace and penitence by the hands of this extraneous evil. It was the curse of mankind that these incongruous fagots were thus bound together—that in the agonized womb of consciousness, these polar twins should be continuously struggling. How, then, were they dissociated?

I was so far in my reflections, when, as I have said, a side light began to shine upon the subject from the laboratory table. I began to perceive more deeply than it has ever yet been stated, the trembling immateriality, the mist-like transience, of this seemingly so solid body in which we walk attired. Certain agents I found to have the power to shake and to pluck back that fleshly vestment, even as a wind might toss the curtains of a pavilion. For two good reasons, I will not enter deeply into this scientific branch of my confession. First, because I have been made to learn that the doom and burthen of our life is bound for ever on man's shoulders; and when the attempt is made to cast it off, it but returns upon us with more unfamiliar and more awful pressure. Second, because, as my narrative will make, alas! too evident, my discoveries were incomplete. Enough, then, that I not only recognized my natural body from the mere aura and effulgence of certain of the powers that made up my spirit, but managed to compound a drug by which these powers should be dethroned from their supremacy, and a second form and countenance substituted, none the less natural to me because they were the expression, and bore the stamp, of lower elements in my soul.

I hesitated long before I put this theory to the test of practice. I knew well that I risked death; for any drug that so potently controlled and shook the very fortress of identity, might by the least scruple of an overdose or at the least inopportunity in the moment of exhibition, utterly blot out that immaterial tabernacle which I looked to it to change. But the temptation of a discovery so singular and profound, at last overcame the suggestions of alarm. I had long since prepared my tincture; I purchased at once, from a firm of wholesale chemists, a large quantity of a particular salt, which I knew, from my experiments, to be the last ingredient required; and, late one accursed night, I compounded the elements, watched them boil and smoke together in the glass, and when the ebullition had subsided, with a strong glow of courage, drank of the potion.

The most racking pangs succeeded: a grinding in the bones, deadly nausea, and a horror of the spirit that cannot be exceeded at the hour of birth or death. Then these agonies began swiftly to subside, and I came to myself as if out of a great sickness. There was something strange in my sensations, something indescribably new, and, from its very novelty, incredibly sweet. I felt younger, lighter, happier in body; within I was conscious of a heady recklessness, a current of disordered sensual images running like a mill-race in my fancy, a solution of the bonds of obligation, an unknown but not an innocent freedom of the soul. I knew myself, at the first breath of this new life, to be more wicked, tenfold more wicked, sold a slave to my original evil; and the thought, in that moment, braced and delighted me like wine. I stretched out my hands, exulting in the freshness of these sensations; and in the act, I was suddenly aware that I had lost in stature.

There was no mirror, at that date, in my room; that which stands beside me as I write was brought there later on, and for the very purpose of those transformations. The night, however, was far gone into the morning—the morning, black as it was, was nearly ripe for the conception of the day—the inmates of my house were locked in the most rigorous hours of slumber; and I determined, flushed as I was with hope and triumph, to venture in my new shape as far as to my bedroom. I crossed the yard, wherein the constellations looked down upon me, I could have thought, with wonder, the first creature of that sort that their unsleeping vigilance had yet disclosed to them; I stole through the corridors, a stranger in my own house; and coming to my room, I saw for the first time the appearance of Edward Hyde.

I must here speak by theory alone, saying not that which I know, but that which I suppose to be most probable. The evil side of my nature, to which I had now transferred the stamping efficacy, was less robust and less developed than the good which I had just deposed. Again, in the course of my life, which had been, after all, nine-tenths a life of effort, virtue, and control, it had been much less exercised and much less exhausted. And hence, as I think, it came about that Edward Hyde was so much smaller, slighter, and younger than Henry Jekyll. Even as good shone upon the countenance of the one, evil was written broadly and plainly on the face of the other. Evil besides (which I must still believe to be the lethal side of man) had left on that body an imprint of deformity and decay. And yet when I looked upon that ugly idol in the glass, I was conscious of no repugnance, rather of a leap of welcome. This, too, was myself. It seemed natural and human. In my eyes it bore a livelier image of the spirit, it seemed more express and single, than the imperfect and divided countenance I had been hitherto accustomed to call mine. And in so far I was doubtless right. I have observed that when I wore the semblance of Edward Hyde, none could come near to me at first without a visible misgiving of the flesh. This, as I take it, was because all human beings, as we meet them, are commingled out of good and evil: and Edward Hyde, alone, in the ranks of mankind, was pure evil.

I lingered but a moment at the mirror: the second and conclusive experiment had yet to be attempted; it yet remained to be seen if I had lost my identity beyond redemption and must flee before daylight from a house that was no longer mine: and hurrying back to my cabinet, I once more prepared and drank the cup, once more suffered the pangs of dissolution, and came to myself once more with the character, the stature, and the face of Henry Jekyll.

That night I had come to the fatal cross roads. Had I approached my discovery in a more noble spirit, had I risked the experiment while under the empire of generous or pious aspirations, all must have been otherwise, and from these agonies of death and birth I had come forth an angel instead of a fiend. The drug had no discriminating action; it was neither diabolical nor divine; it but shook the doors of the prison-house of my disposition; and, like the captives of Philippi, that which stood within ran forth. At that time my virtue slumbered; my evil, kept awake by ambition, was alert and swift to seize the occasion; and the thing that was projected was Edward Hyde. Hence, although I had now two characters as well as two appearances, one was wholly evil, and the other was still the old Henry Jekyll, that incongruous compound of whose reformation and improvement I had already learned to despair. The movement was thus wholly toward the worse.

Even at that time, I had not yet conquered my aversion to the dryness of a life of study. I would still be merrily disposed at times; and as my pleasures were (to say the least) undignified, and I was not only well known and highly considered, but growing towards the elderly man, this incoherency of my life was daily growing more unwelcome. It was on this side that my new power tempted me until I fell in slavery. I had but to drink the cup, to doff at once the body of the noted professor, and to assume, like a thick cloak, that of Edward Hyde. I smiled at the notion; it seemed to me at the time to be humorous; I made my preparations with the most studious care. I took and furnished that house in Soho, to which Hyde was tracked by the police; and engaged as housekeeper a creature whom I well knew to be silent and unscrupulous. On the other side, I announced to my servants that a Mr Hyde (whom I described) was to have full liberty and power about my house in the square; and, to parry mishaps, I even called and made myself a familiar object, in my second character. I next drew up that will to which you so much objected; so that if anything befell me in the person of Dr Jekyll, I could enter on that of Edward Hyde without pecuniary loss. And thus fortified, as I supposed, on every side, I began to profit by the strange immunities of my position.

Men have before hired bravos to transact their crimes, while their own person and reputation sat under shelter. I was the first that ever did so for his pleasures. I was the first that could thus plod in the public eye with a load of genial respectability, and in a moment, like a schoolboy, strip off these lendings and spring headlong into the sea of liberty. But for me, in my impenetrable mantle, the safety was complete. Think of it—I did not even exist! Let me but escape into my laboratory door, give me but a second or two to mix and swallow the draught that I had always standing ready; and, whatever he had done, Edward Hyde would pass away like the stain of breath upon a mirror; and there in his stead, quietly at home, trimming the midnight lamp in his study, a man who could afford to laugh at suspicion, would be Henry Jekyll.

The pleasures which I made haste to seek in my disguise were, as I have said, undignified; I would scarce use a harder term. But in the hands of Edward Hyde, they soon began to turn towards the monstrous. When I would come back from these excursions, I was often plunged into a kind of wonder at my vicarious depravity. This familiar that I called out of my own soul, and sent forth alone to do his good pleasure, was a being inherently malign and villainous; his every act and thought centred on self; drinking pleasure with bestial avidity from any degree of torture to another; relentless like a man of stone. Henry Jekyll stood at times aghast before the acts of Edward Hyde; but the situation was apart from ordinary laws, and insidiously relaxed the grasp of conscience. It was Hyde, after all, and Hyde alone, that was guilty. Jekyll was no worse; he woke again to his good qualities seemingly unimpaired; he would even make haste, where it was possible, to undo the evil done by Hyde. And thus his conscience slumbered.

Into the details of the infamy at which I thus connived (for even now I can scarce grant that I committed it) I have no design of entering. I mean but to point out the warnings and the successive steps with which my chastisement approached. I met with one accident which, as it brought on no consequence, I shall no more than mention. An act of cruelty to a child aroused against me the anger of a passer-by, whom I recognized the other day in the person of your kinsman; the doctor and the child's family joined him; there were moments when I feared for my life; and at last, in order to pacify their too just resentment, Edward Hyde had to bring them to the door, and pay them in a cheque drawn in the name of Henry Jekyll. But this danger was easily eliminated from the future, by opening an account at another bank in the name of Edward Hyde himself; and when, by sloping my own hand backwards, I had supplied my double with a signature, I thought I sat beyond the reach of fate.

Some two months before the murder of Sir Danvers, I had been out for one of my adventures, had returned at a late hour, and woke the next day in bed with somewhat odd sensations. It was in vain I looked about me; in vain I saw the decent furniture and tall proportions of my room in the square; in vain that I recognized the pattern of the bed curtains and the design of the mahogany frame; something still kept insisting that I was not where I was, that I had not wakened where I seemed to be, but in the little room in Soho where I was accustomed to sleep in the body of Edward Hyde. I smiled to myself, and, in my psychological way, began lazily to inquire into the elements of this illusion, occasionally, even as I did so, dropping back into a comfortable morning doze. I was still so engaged when, on one of my more wakeful moments, my eye fell upon my hand. Now, the hand of Henry Jekyll (as you have often remarked) was professional in shape and size; it was large, firm, white, and comely. But the hand which I now saw, clearly enough in the yellow light of a mid-London morning, lying half shut on the bedclothes, was lean, corded, knuckly, of a dusky pallor, and thickly shaded with a swart growth of hair. It was the hand of Edward Hyde.

I must have stared upon it for near half a minute, sunk as I was in the mere stupidity of wonder, before terror woke up in my breast as sudden and startling as the crash of cymbals; and bounding from my bed, I rushed to the mirror. At the sight that met my eyes, my blood was changed into something exquisitely thin and icy. Yes, I had gone to bed Henry Jekyll, I had awakened Edward Hyde. How was this to be explained? I asked myself; and then, with another bound of terror—how was it to be remedied? It was well on in the morning; the servants were up; all my drugs were in the cabinet—a long journey, down two pair of stairs, through the back passage, across the open court and through the anatomical theatre, from where I was then standing horror-struck. It might indeed be possible to cover my face; but of what use was that, when I was unable to conceal the alteration in my stature? And then, with an over-powering sweetness of relief, it came back upon my mind that the servants were already used to the coming and going of my second self. I had soon dressed, as well as I was able, in clothes of my own size; had soon passed through the house, where Bradshaw stared and drew back at seeing Mr Hyde at such an hour and in such a strange array; and ten minutes later, Dr Jekyll had returned to his own shape, and was sitting down, with a darkened brow, to make a feint of breakfasting.

Small indeed was my appetite. This inexplicable incident, this reversal of my previous experience, seemed, like the Babylonian finger on the wall, to be spelling out the letters of my judgement; and I began to reflect more seriously than ever before on the issues and possibilities of my double existence. That part of me which I had the power of projecting had lately been much exercised and nourished; it had seemed to me of late as though the body of Edward Hyde had grown in stature, as though (when I wore that form) I were conscious of a more generous tide of blood; and I began to spy danger that, if this were much prolonged, the balance of my nature might be permanently overthrown, the power of voluntary change be forfeited, and the character of Edward Hyde become irrevocably mine. The power of the drug had not been always equally displayed. Once, very early in my career, it had totally failed me; since then I had been obliged on more than one occasion to double, and once, with infinite risk of death, to treble the amount; and these rare uncertainties had cast hitherto the sole shadow on my contentment. Now, however, and in the light of that morning's accident, I was led to remark that whereas, in the beginning, the difficulty had been to throw off the body of Jekyll, it had of late gradually but decidedly transferred itself to the other side. All things therefore seemed to point to this: that I was slowly losing hold of my original and better self, and becoming slowly incorporated with my second and worse.

Between these two, I now felt I had to choose. My two natures had memory in common, but all other faculties were most unequally shared between them. Jekyll (who was composite) now with the most sensitive apprehension, now with a greedy gusto, projected and shared in the pleasures and adventures of Hyde; but Hyde was indifferent to Jekyll, or but remembered him as the mountain bandit remembers the cavern in which he conceals himself from pursuit. Jekyll had more than a father's interest; Hyde had more than a son's indifference. To cast in my lot with Jekyll was to die to those appetites which I had long secretly indulged and had of late begun to pamper. To cast it in with Hyde was to die to a thousand interests and aspirations, and to become, at a blow and for ever, despised and friendless. The bargain might appear unequal; but there was still another consideration in the scales; for while Jekyll would suffer smartingly in the fires of abstinence, Hyde would not be even conscious of all that he had lost. Strange as my circumstances were, the terms of this debate are as old and commonplace as man; much the same inducements and alarms cast the die for any tempted and trembling sinner; and it fell out with me, as it falls with so vast a majority of my fellows, that I chose the better part, and was found wanting in the strength to keep to it.

Yes, I preferred the elderly and discontented doctor, surrounded by friends, and cherishing honest hopes, and bade a resolute farewell to the liberty, the comparative youth, the light step, leaping pulses, and secret pleasures, that I had enjoyed in the disguise of Hyde. I made this choice perhaps with some unconscious reservation, for I neither gave up the house in Soho, nor destroyed the clothes of Edward Hyde, which still lay ready in my cabinet. For two months, however, I was true to my determination; for two months I led a life of such severity as I had never before attained to, and enjoyed the compensations of an approving conscience. But time began at last to obliterate the freshness of my alarm; the praises of conscience began to grow into a thing of course; I began to be tortured with throes and longings, as of Hyde struggling after freedom; and at last, in an hour of moral weakness, I once again compounded and swallowed the transforming draught. I do not suppose that when a drunkard reasons with himself upon his vice, he is once out of five hundred times affected by the dangers that he runs through his brutish physical insensibility; neither had I, long as I had considered my position, made enough allowance for the complete moral insensibility and insensate readiness to evil, which were the leading characters of Edward Hyde. Yet it was by these that I was punished. My devil had been long caged, he came out roaring. I was conscious, even when I took the draught, of a more unbridled, a more furious propensity to ill. It must have been this, I suppose, that stirred in my soul that tempest of impatience with which I listened to the civilities of my unhappy victim; I declare at least, before God, no man morally sane could have been guilty of that crime upon so pitiful a provocation; and that I struck in no more reasonable spirit than that in which a sick child may break a plaything. But I had voluntarily stripped myself of all those balancing instincts by which even the worst of us continues to walk with some degree of steadiness among temptations; and in my case, to be tempted, however slightly, was to fall.

Instantly the spirit of hell awoke in me and raged. With a transport of glee, I mauled the unresisting body, tasting delight from every blow; and it was not till weariness had begun to succeed that I was suddenly, in the top fit of my delirium, struck through the heart by a cold thrill of terror. A mist dispersed; I saw my life to be forfeit; and fled from the scene of these excesses, at once glorying and trembling, my lust of evil gratified and stimulated, my love of life screwed to the topmost peg. I ran to the house in Soho, and (to make assurance doubly sure) destroyed my papers; thence I set out through the lamplit streets, in the same divided ecstasy of mind, gloating on my crime, lightheadedly devising others in the future, and yet still hastening and still hearkening in my wake for the steps of the avenger. Hyde had a song upon his lips as he compounded the draught, and as he drank it pledged the dead man. The pangs of transformation had not done tearing him, before Henry Jekyll, with streaming tears of gratitude and remorse, had fallen upon his knees and lifted his clasped hands to God. The veil of self-indulgence was rent from head to foot, I saw my life as a whole: I followed it up from the days of childhood, when I had walked with my father's hand, and through the self-denying toils of my professional life, to arrive again and again, with the same sense of unreality, at the damned horrors of the evening. I could have screamed aloud; I sought with tears and prayers to smother down the crowd of hideous images and sounds with which my memory swarmed against me; and still, between the petitions, the ugly face of my iniquity stared into my soul. As the acuteness of this remorse began to die away, it was succeeded by a sense of joy. The problem of my conduct was solved. Hyde was thenceforth impossible; whether I would or not, I was now confined to the better part of my existence; and oh, how I rejoiced to think it! with what willing humility embraced anew the restrictions of natural life! with what sincere renunciation I locked the door by which I had so often gone and come, and ground the key under my heel!

The next day came the news that the murder had been overlooked, that the guilt of Hyde was patent to the world, and that the victim was a man high in public estimation. It was not only a crime, it had been a tragic folly. I think I was glad to know it; I think I was glad to have my better impulses thus buttressed and guarded by the terrors of the scaffold. Jekyll was now my city of refuge; let but Hyde peep out an instant, and the hands of all men would be raised to take and slay him.

I resolved in my future conduct to redeem the past; and I can say with honesty that my resolve was fruitful of some good. You know yourself how earnestly in the last months of last year I laboured to relieve suffering; you know that much was done for others, and that the days passed quietly, almost happily for myself. Nor can I truly say that I wearied of this beneficent and innocent life; I think instead that I daily enjoyed it more completely: but I was still cursed with my duality of purpose; and as the first edge of my penitence wore off, the lower side of me, so long indulged, so recently chained down, began to growl for license. Not that I dreamed of resuscitating Hyde; the bare idea of that would startle me to frenzy: no, it was in my own person that I was once more tempted to trifle with my conscience; and it was as an ordinary secret sinner that I at last fell before the assaults of temptation.

There comes an end to all things; the most capacious measure is filled at last; and this brief condescension to my evil finally destroyed the balance of my soul. And yet I was not alarmed; the fall seemed natural, like a return to the old days before I had made my discovery. It was a fine, clear January day, wet under foot where the frost had melted, but cloudless overhead; and the Regent's Park was full of winter chirrupings and sweet with spring odours. I sat in the sun on a bench; the animal within me licking the chops of memory; the spiritual side a little drowsed, promising subsequent penitence, but not yet moved to begin. After all, I reflected, I was like my neighbours; and then I smiled, comparing myself with other men, comparing my active goodwill with the lazy cruelty of their neglect. And at the very moment of that vainglorious thought, a qualm came over me, a horrid nausea and the most deadly shuddering. These passed away, and left me faint; and then as in its turn the faintness subsided, I began to be aware of a change in the temper of my thoughts, a greater boldness, a contempt of danger, a solution of the bonds of obligation. I looked down; my clothes hung formlessly on my shrunken limbs; the hand that lay on my knee was corded and hairy. I was once more Edward Hyde. A moment before I had been safe of all men's respect, wealthy, beloved—the cloth laying for me in the dining-room at home; and now I was the common quarry of mankind, hunted, houseless, a known murderer, thrall to the gallows.

My reason wavered, but it did not fail me utterly. I have more than once observed that, in my second character, my faculties seemed sharpened to a point and my spirits more tensely elastic; thus it came about that, where Jekyll perhaps might have succumbed, Hyde rose to the importance of the moment. My drugs were in one of the presses of my cabinet: how was I to reach them? That was the problem that (crushing my temples in my hands) I set myself to solve. The laboratory door I had closed. If I sought to enter by the house, my own servants would consign me to the gallows. I saw I must employ another hand, and thought of Lanyon. How was he to be reached? how persuaded? Supposing that I escaped capture in the streets, how was I to make my way into his presence? and how should I, an unknown and displeasing visitor, prevail on the famous physician to rifle the study of his colleague, Dr Jekyll? Then I remembered that of my original character one part remained to me: I could write my own hand; and once I had conceived that kindling spark, the way that I must follow became lighted up from end to end.

Thereupon, I arranged my clothes as best I could, and summoning a passing hansom, drove to an hotel in Portland Street, the name of which I chanced to remember. At my appearance (which was indeed comical enough, however tragic a fate these garments covered) the driver could not conceal his mirth. I gnashed my teeth upon him with a gust of devilish fury; and the smile withered from his face—happily for him—yet more happily for myself, for in another instant I had certainly dragged him from his perch. At the inn, as I entered, I looked about me with so black a countenance as made the attendants tremble; not a look did they exchange in my presence; but obsequiously took my orders, led me to a private room, and brought me wherewithal to write. Hyde in danger of his life was a creature new to me: shaken with inordinate anger, strung to the pitch of murder, lusting to inflict pain. Yet the creature was astute; mastered his fury with a great effort of the will; composed his two important letters, one to Lanyon and one to Poole, and, that he might receive actual evidence of their being posted, sent them out with directions that they should be registered.

Thenceforward, he sat all day over the fire in the private room, gnawing his nails; there he dined, sitting alone with his fears, the waiter visibly quailing before his eye; and thence, when the night was fully come, he set forth in the corner of a closed cab, and was driven to and fro about the streets of the city. He, I say—I cannot say, I. That child of Hell had nothing human; nothing lived in him but fear and hatred. And when at last, thinking the driver had begun to grow suspicious, he discharged the cab and ventured on foot, attired in his misfitting clothes, an object marked out for observation, into the midst of the nocturnal passengers, these two base passions raged within him like a tempest. He walked fast, haunted by his fears, chattering to himself, skulking through the less frequented thoroughfares, counting the minutes that still divided him from midnight. Once a woman spoke to him, offering, I think, a box of lights. He smote her in the face, and she fled.

When I came to myself at Lanyon's, the horror of my old friend perhaps affected me somewhat: I do not know; it was at least but a drop in the sea to the abhorrence with which I looked back upon these hours. A change had come over me. It was no longer the fear of the gallows, it was the horror of being Hyde that racked me. I received Lanyon's condemnation partly in a dream; it was partly in a dream that I came home to my own house and got into bed. I slept after the prostration of the day, with a stringent and profound slumber which not even the nightmares that wrung me could avail to break. I awoke in the morning shaken, weakened, but refreshed. I still hated and feared the thought of the brute that slept within me, and I had not of course forgotten the appalling dangers of the day before; but I was once more at home, in my own house and close to my drugs; and gratitude for my escape shone so strong in my soul that it almost rivalled the brightness of hope.

I was stepping leisurely across the court after breakfast, drinking the chill of the air with pleasure, when I was seized again with those indescribable sensations that heralded the change; and I had but the time to gain the shelter of my cabinet, before I was once again raging and freezing with the passions of Hyde. It took on this occasion a double dose to recall me to myself; and, alas! six hours after as I sat looking sadly in the fire, the pangs returned, and the drug had to be re-administered. In short, from that day forth it seemed only by a great effort as of gymnastics, and only under the immediate stimulation of the drug, that I was able to wear the countenance of Jekyll. At all hours of the day and night I would be taken with the premonitory shudder; above all, if I slept, or even dozed for a moment in my chair, it was always as Hyde that I awakened. Under the strain of this continually impending doom, and by the sleeplessness to which I now condemned myself, aye, even beyond what I had thought possible to man, I became, in my own person, a creature eaten up and emptied by fever, languidly weak both in body and mind, and solely occupied by one thought: the horror of my other self. But when I slept, or when the virtue of the medicine wore off, I would leap almost without transition (for the pangs of transformation grew daily less marked) into the possession of a fancy brimming with images of terror, a soul boiling with causeless hatreds, and a body that seemed not strong enough to contain the raging energies of life. The powers of Hyde seemed to have grown with the sickliness of Jekyll. And certainly the hate that now divided them was equal on each side. With Jekyll, it was a thing of vital instinct. He had now seen the full deformity of that creature that shared with him some of the phenomena of consciousness, and was co-heir with him to death; and beyond these links of community, which in themselves made the most poignant part of his distress, he thought of Hyde, for all his energy of life, as of something not only hellish but inorganic. This was the shocking thing; that the slime of the pit seemed to utter cries and voices; that the amorphous dust gesticulated and sinned; that what was dead, and had no shape, should usurp the offices of life. And this again, that that insurgent horror was knit to him closer than a wife, closer than an eye; lay caged in his flesh, where he heard it mutter and felt it struggle to be born; and at every hour of weakness, and in the confidence of slumber, prevailed against him, and deposed him out of life. The hatred of Hyde for Jekyll was of a different order. His terror of the gallows drove him continually to commit temporary suicide, and return to his subordinate station of a part instead of a person; but he loathed the necessity, he loathed the despondency into which Jekyll was now fallen, and he resented the dislike with which he was himself regarded. Hence the ape-like tricks that he would play me, scrawling in my own hand blasphemies on the pages of my books, burning the letters and destroying the portrait of my father; and indeed, had it not been for his fear of death, he would long ago have ruined himself in order to involve me in the ruin. But his love of life is wonderful; I go further; I, who sicken and freeze at the mere thought of him, when I recall the abjection and passion of this attachment, and when I know how he fears my power to cut him off by suicide, I find it in my heart to pity him.

It is useless, and the time awfully fails me, to prolong this description; no one has ever suffered such torments, let that suffice; and yet even to these, habit brought—no, not alleviation—but a certain callousness of soul, a certain acquiescence of despair; and my punishment might have gone on for years, but for the last calamity which has now fallen, and which has finally severed me from my own face and nature. My provision of the salt, which had never been renewed since the date of the first experiment, began to run low. I sent out for a fresh supply, and mixed the draught; the ebullition followed, and the first change of colour, not the second; I drank it, and it was without efficacy. You will learn from Poole how I have had London ransacked: it was in vain; and I am now persuaded that my first supply was impure, and that it was that unknown impurity which lent efficacy to the draught.

About a week has passed, and I am now finishing this statement under the influence of the last of the old powders. This, then, is the last time, short of a miracle, that Henry Jekyll can think his own thoughts or see his own face (now how sadly altered!) in the glass. Nor must I delay too long to bring my writing to an end; for if my narrative has hitherto escaped destruction, it has been by a combination of great prudence and great good luck. Should the throes of change take me in the act of writing it, Hyde will tear it in pieces; but if some time shall have elapsed after I have laid it by, his wonderful selfishness and circumscription to the moment will probably save it once again from the action of his ape-like spite. And, indeed, the doom that is closing on us both has already changed and crushed him. Half an hour from now, when I shall again and for ever reindue that hated personality, I know how I shall sit shuddering and weeping in my chair, or continue, with the most strained and fear-struck ecstasy of listening, to pace up and down this room (my last earthly refuge) and give ear to every sound of menace. Will Hyde die upon the scaffold? or will he find the courage to release himself at the last moment? God knows; I am careless; this is my true hour of death, and what is to follow concerns another than myself. Here, then, as I lay down the pen, and proceed to seal up my confession, I bring the life of that unhappy Henry Jekyll to an end.

THE SUICIDE CLUB

1

Story of the Young Man with the Cream Tarts

During his residence in London, the accomplished Prince Florizel of Bohemia gained the affection of all classes by the seduction of his manner and by a well-considered generosity. He was a remarkable man even by what was known of him; and that was but a small part of what he actually did. Although of a placid temper in ordinary circumstances, and accustomed to take the world with as much philosophy as any ploughman, the Prince of Bohemia was not without a taste for ways of life more adventurous and eccentric than that to which he was destined by his birth. Now and then, when he fell into a low humour, when there was no laughable play to witness in any of the London theatres, and when the season of the year was unsuitable to those field sports in which he excelled all competitors, he would summon his confidant and Master of the Horse, Colonel Geraldine, and bid him prepare himself against an evening ramble. The Master of the Horse was a young officer of a brave and even temerarious disposition. He greeted the news with delight, and hastened to make ready. Long practice and a varied acquaintance of life had given him a singular facility in disguise; he could adapt not only his face and bearing, but his voice and almost his thoughts, to those of any rank, character, or nation; and in this way he diverted attention from the Prince, and sometimes gained admission for the pair into strange societies. The civil authorities were never taken into the secret of these adventures; the imperturbable courage of the one and the ready invention and chivalrous devotion of the other had brought them through a score of dangerous passes; and they grew in confidence as time went on.

One evening in March they were driven by a sharp fall of sleet into an Oyster Bar in the immediate neighbourhood of Leicester Square. Colonel Geraldine was dressed and painted to represent a person connected with the Press in reduced circumstances; while the Prince had, as usual, travestied his appearance by the addition of false whiskers and a pair of large adhesive eyebrows. These lent him a shaggy and weather-beaten air, which, for one of his urbanity, formed the most impenetrable disguise. Thus equipped, the commander and his satellite sipped their brandy and soda in security.

The bar was full of guests, male and female; but though more than one of these offered to fall into talk with our adventurers, none of them promised to grow interesting upon a nearer acquaintance. There was nothing present but the lees of London and the commonplace of disrespectability; and the Prince had already fallen to yawning, and was beginning to grow weary of the whole excursion, when the swing doors were pushed violently open, and a young man, followed by a couple of commissionaires, entered the bar. Each of the commissionaires carried a large dish of cream tarts under a cover, which they at once removed; and the young man made the round of the company, and pressed these confections upon every one's acceptance with an exaggerated courtesy. Sometimes his offer was laughingly accepted; sometimes it was firmly, or even harshly, rejected. In these latter cases the new-comer always ate the tart himself, with some more or less humorous commentary.

At last he accosted Prince Florizel.

"Sir," said he, with a profound obeisance, proffering the tart at the same time between his thumb and forefinger, "will you so far honour an entire stranger? I can answer for the quality of the pastry, having eaten two dozen and three of them myself since five o'clock."

"I am in the habit," replied the Prince, "of looking not so much to the nature of a gift as to the spirit in which it is offered."

"The spirit, sir," returned the young man, with another bow, "is one of mockery."

"Mockery?" repeated Florizel. "And whom do you propose to mock?"

"I am not here to expound my philosophy," replied the other, "but to distribute these cream tarts. If I mention that I heartily include myself in the ridicule of the transaction, I hope you will consider honour satisfied and condescend. If not, you will constrain me to eat my twenty-eighth, and I own to being weary of the exercise."

"You touch me," said the Prince, "and I have all the will in the world to rescue you from this dilemma, but upon one condition. If my friend and I eat your cakes—for which we have neither of us any natural inclination—we shall expect you to join us at supper by way of recompense."

The young man seemed to reflect.

"I have still several dozen upon hand," he said at last; "and that will make it necessary for me to visit several more bars before my great affair is concluded. This will take some time; and if you are hungry—"

The Prince interrupted him with a polite gesture.

"My friend and I will accompany you," he said; "for we have already a deep interest in your very agreeable mode of passing an evening. And now that the preliminaries of peace are settled, allow me to sign the treaty for both."

And the Prince swallowed the tart with the best grace imaginable.

"It is delicious," said he.

"I perceive you are a connoisseur," replied the young man.

Colonel Geraldine likewise did honour to the pastry; and every one in that bar having now either accepted or refused his delicacies, the young man with the cream tarts led the way to another and similar establishment. The two commissionaires, who seemed to have grown accustomed to their absurd employment, followed immediately after; and the Prince and the Colonel brought up the rear, arm in arm, and smiling to each other as they went. In this order the company visited two other taverns, where scenes were enacted of a like nature to that already described—some refusing, some accepting, the favours of this vagabond hospitality, and the young man himself eating each rejected tart.

On leaving the third saloon the young man counted his store. There were but nine remaining, three in one tray and six in the other.

"Gentlemen," said he, addressing himself to his two

new followers, "I am unwilling to delay your supper. I am positively sure you must be hungry. I feel that I owe you a special consideration. And on this great day for me, when I am closing a career of folly by my most conspicuously silly action, I wish to behave handsomely to all who give me countenance. Gentlemen, you shall wait no longer. Although my constitution is shattered by previous excesses, at the risk of my life I liquidate the suspensory condition."

With these words he crushed the nine remaining tarts into his mouth, and swallowed them at a single movement each. Then, turning to the commissionaires, he gave them a couple of sovereigns. "I have to thank you," said he, "for your extraordinary patience."

And he dismissed them with a bow apiece. For some seconds he stood looking at the purse from which he had just paid his assistants, then, with a laugh, he tossed it into the middle of the street, and signified his readiness for supper.

In a small French restaurant in Soho, which had enjoyed an exaggerated reputation for some little while, but had already begun to be forgotten, and in a private room up two pair of stairs, the three companions made a very elegant supper, and drank three or four bottles of champagne, talking the while upon indifferent subjects. The young man was fluent and gay, but he laughed louder than was natural in a person of polite breeding; his hands trembled violently, and his voice took sudden and surprising inflections, which seemed to be independent of his will. The dessert had been cleared away, and all three had lighted their cigars, when the Prince addressed him in these words:

"You will, I am sure, pardon my curiosity. What I

have seen of you has greatly pleased but even more puzzled me. And though I should be loth to seem indiscreet, I must tell you that my friend and I are persons very well worthy to be entrusted with a secret. We have many of our own, which we are continually revealing to improper ears. And if, as I suppose, your story is a silly one, you need have no delicacy with us, who are two of the silliest men in England. My name is Godall, Theophilus Godall; my friend is Major Alfred Hammersmith—or at least, such is the name by which he chooses to be known. We pass our lives entirely in the search for extravagant adventures; and there is no extravagance with which we are not capable of sympathy."

"I like you, Mr Godall," returned the young man; "you inspire me with a natural confidence; and I have not the slightest objection to your friend the Major, whom I take to be a nobleman in masquerade. At least, I am sure he is no soldier."

The Colonel smiled at this compliment to the perfection of his art; and the young man went on in a more animated manner.

"There is every reason why I should not tell you my story. Perhaps that is just the reason why I am going to do so. At least, you seem so well prepared to hear a tale of silliness that I cannot find it in my heart to disappoint you. My name, in spite of your example, I shall keep to myself. My age is not essential to the narrative. I am descended from my ancestors by ordinary generation, and from them I inherited the very eligible human tenement which I still occupy, and a fortune of three hundred pounds a year. I suppose they also handed on to me a hare-brain humour, which it has been my chief delight to indulge. I received a good education. I can play the violin nearly well enough to earn money in the orchestra of a penny gaff, but not quite. The same remark applies to the flute and the French horn. I learned enough of whist to lose about a hundred a year at that scientific game. My acquaintance with French was sufficient to enable me to squander money in Paris with almost the same facility as in London. In short, I am a person full of manly accomplishments. I have had every sort of adventure, including a duel about nothing. Only two months ago I met a young lady exactly suited to my taste in mind and body; I found my heart melt; I saw that I had come upon my fate at last, and was in the way to fall in love. But when I came to reckon up what remained to me of my capital, I found it amounted to something less than four hundred pounds! I ask you fairly—can a man who respects himself fall in love on four hundred pounds? I concluded, certainly not; left the presence of my charmer, and slightly accelerating my usual rate of expenditure, came this morning to my last eighty pounds. This I divided into two equal parts; forty I reserved for a particular purpose; the remaining forty I was to dissipate before the night. I have passed a very entertaining day, and played many farces besides that of the cream tarts which procured me the advantage of your acquaintance; for I was determined, as I told you, to bring a foolish career to a still more foolish conclusion; and when you saw me throw my purse into the street the forty pounds were at an end. Now you know me as well as I know myself: a fool but consistent in his folly; and, as I will ask you to believe, neither a whimperer nor a coward."

From the whole tone of the young man's statement it

was plain that he harboured very bitter and contemptuous thoughts about himself. His auditors were led to imagine that his love affair was nearer his heart than he admitted, and that he had a design on his own life. The farce of the cream tarts began to have very much the air of a tragedy in disguise.

"Why, is this not odd," broke out Geraldine, giving a look to Prince Florizel "that we three fellows should have met by the merest accident in so large a wilderness as London, and should be so nearly in the same condition?"

"How?" cried the young man. "Are you, too, ruined? Is this supper a folly like my cream tarts? Has the devil brought three of his own together for a last carouse?"

"The devil, depend upon it, can sometimes do a very gentlemanly thing," returned Prince Florizel; "and I am so much touched by this coincidence, that, although we are not entirely in the same case, I am going to put an end to the disparity. Let your heroic treatment of the last cream tarts be my example."

So saying, the Prince drew out his purse and took from it a small bundle of bank-notes.

"You see, I was a week or so behind you, but I mean to catch you up and come neck and neck into the winning-post," he continued. "This," laying one of the notes upon the table, "will suffice for the bill. As for the rest—"

He tossed them into the fire, and they went up the chimney in a single blaze.

The young man tried to catch his arm, but as the table was between them his interference came too late.

"Unhappy man," he cried, "you should not have burned them all! You should have kept forty pounds."

Story of the Young Man with the Cream Tarts

"Forty pounds!" repeated the Prince. "Why, in Heaven's name, forty pounds?"

"Why not eighty?" cried the Colonel; "for to my certain knowledge there must have been a hundred in the bundle."

"It was only forty pounds he needed," said the young man gloomily. "But without them there is no admission. The rule is strict. Forty pounds for each. Accursed life, where a man cannot even die without money!"

The Prince and the Colonel exchanged glances.

"Explain yourself," said the latter. "I have still a pocket book tolerably well lined, and I need not say how readily I should share my wealth with Godall. But I must know to what end: you must certainly tell us what you mean."

The young man seemed to awaken; he looked uneasily from one to the other, and his face flushed deeply.

"You are not fooling me?" he asked. "You are indeed ruined men like me?"

"Indeed, I am for my part," replied the Colonel.

"And for mine," said the Prince, "I have given you proof. Who but a ruined man would throw his notes into the fire? The action speaks for itself."

"A ruined man—yes," returned the other suspiciously, "or else a millionaire."

"Enough, sir," said the Prince; "I have said so, and I am not accustomed to have my word remain in doubt."

"Ruined?" said the young man. "Are you ruined, like me? Are you, after a life of indulgence, come to such a pass that you can only indulge yourself one thing more? Are you"—he kept lowering his voice as he went on—"are you going to give yourselves that last indulgence? Are you going to avoid the consequences of your folly by the one infallible and easy path? Are you going to give the slip to the sheriff's officers of conscience by the one open door?"

Suddenly he broke off and attempted to laugh.

"Here is your health!" he cried, emptying his glass, "and good night to you, my merry ruined men."

Colonel caught him by the arm as he was about to rise.

"You lack confidence in us," he said, "and you are wrong. To all your questions I make answer in the affirmative. But I am not so timid, and can speak the Queen's English plainly. We too, like yourself, have had enough of life, and are determined to die. Sooner or later, alone or together, we meant to seek out Death and beard him where he lies ready. Since we have met you, and your case is more pressing, let it be tonight— and at once—and, if you will, all three together. Such a penniless trio," he cried, "should go arm in arm into the halls of Pluto, and give each other some countenance among the shades!"

Geraldine had hit exactly on the manners and intonations that became the part he was playing. The Prince himself was disturbed, and looked over at his confidant with a shade of doubt. As for the young man, the flush came back darkly into his cheek, and his eyes threw out a spark of light.

"You are the men for me!" he cried, with an almost terrible gaiety. "Shake hands upon the bargain!" (his hand was cold and wet). "You little know in what a company you will begin the march! You little know in what a happy moment for yourselves you partook of my cream tarts! I am only a unit, but I am a unit in an army. I know Death's private door. I am one of his familiars, and can show you into eternity without ceremony and yet without scandal.

They called upon him eagerly to explain his meaning.

"Can you muster eighty pounds between you?" he demanded.

Geraldine ostentatiously consulted his pocket book, and replied in the affirmative.

"Fortunate beings!" cried the young man. "Forty pounds is the entry money of the Suicide Club."

"The Suicide Club," said the Prince, "why, what the devil is that?"

"Listen," said the young man; "this is the age of conveniences, and I have to tell you of the last perfection of the sort. We have affairs in different places; and hence railways were invented. Railways separated us infallibly from our friends; and so telegraphs were made that we might communicate speedily at great distances. Even in hotels we have lifts to spare us a climb of some hundred steps. Now, we know that life is only a stage to play the fool upon as long as the part amuses us. There was one more convenience lacking to modern comfort; a decent easy way to quit that stage; the back stairs to liberty, or, as I said this moment, Death's private door. This, my two fellow rebels, is supplied by the Suicide Club. Do not suppose that you and I are alone, or even exceptional, in the highly reasonable desire that we profess. A large number of our fellow men, who have grown heartily sick of the performance in which they are expected to join daily and all their lives long, are only kept from flight by one or two considerations. Some have families who would be shocked, or even blamed, if the matter became public; others have a weakness at heart and recoil from the circumstances of death. That is, to some extent, my own experience. I cannot put a pistol to my head and draw the trigger; for something stronger than myself withholds the act; and although I loathe life, I have not strength enough in my body to take hold of death and be done with it. For such as I and for all who desire to be out of the coil without posthumous scandal, the Suicide Club has been inaugurated. How this has been managed, what is its history, or what may be its ramifications in other lands, I am myself uninformed; and what I know of its constitution, I am not at liberty to communicate to you. To this extent, however, I am at your service. If you are truly tired of life, I will introduce you tonight to a meeting; and if not tonight, at least some time within the week, you will be easily relieved of your existences. It is now (consulting his watch) eleven; by half-past, at latest, we must leave this place; so that you have half an hour before you to consider my proposal. It is more serious than a cream tart," he added, with a smile; "and I suspect more palatable."

"More serious, certainly," returned Colonel Geraldine; 'and as it is so much more so, will you allow me five minutes' speech in private with my friend, Mr Godall?"

"It is only fair," answered the young man. "If you will permit, I will retire."

"You will be very obliging," said the Colonel.

As soon as the two were alone—"What," said Prince Florizel "is the use of this confabulation, Geraldine? I see you are flurried, whereas my mind is very tranquilly made up. I will see the end of this."

"Your Highness," said the Colonel, turning pale; "let me ask you to consider the importance of your life, not only to your friends, but to the public interest. 'If not tonight,' said this madman; but supposing that tonight some irreparable disaster were to overtake your Highness's person, what, let me ask you, what would be my despair, and what the concern and disaster of a great nation?"

"I will see the end of this," repeated the Prince in his most deliberate tones; "and have the kindness, Colonel Geraldine, to remember and respect your word of honour as a gentleman. Under no circumstances, recollect, nor without my special authority, are you to betray the incognito under which I choose to go abroad. These were my commands, which I now reiterate. And now," he added, "let me ask you to call for the bill"

Colonel Geraldine bowed in submission; but he had a very white face as he summoned the young man of the cream tarts, and issued his directions to the waiter. The Prince preserved his undisturbed demeanour, and described a Palais Royal farce to the young suicide with great humour and gusto. He avoided the Colonel's appealing looks without ostentation, and selected another cheroot with more than usual care. Indeed, he was now the only man of the party who kept any command over his nerves.

The bill was discharged, the Prince giving the whole change of the note to the astonished waiter; and the three drove off in a four-wheeler. They were not long upon the way before the cab stopped at the entrance to a rather dark court. Here all descended.

After Geraldine had paid the fare, the young man turned, and addressed Prince Florizel as follows:

"It is still time, Mr Godall, to make good your escape into thraldom. And for you, too, Major Hammersmith. Reflect well before you take another step; and if your hearts say no—here are the crossroads."

"Lead on, sir," said the Prince. "I am not the man to go back from a thing once said."

"Your coolness does me good," replied their guide. "I have never seen anyone so unmoved at this conjuncture; and yet you are not the first whom I have escorted to this door. More than one of my friends has preceded me, where I knew I must shortly follow. But this is of no interest to you. Wait for me here only a few moments; I shall return as soon as I have arranged the preliminaries of your introduction."

And with that the young man, waving his hand to his companions, turned into the court, entered a doorway, and disappeared.

"Of all our follies," said Colonel in a low voice, "this is the wildest and most dangerous."

"I perfectly believe so," returned the Prince.

"We have still," pursued the Colonel, "a moment to ourselves. Let me beseech your Highness to profit by the opportunity and retire. The consequences of this step are so dark, and may be so grave, that I feel myself justified in pushing a little further than usual the liberty which your Highness is so condescending as to allow me in private.

"Am I to understand that Colonel Geraldine is afraid?" asked his Highness, taking his cheroot from his lips, and looking keenly into the other's face.

"My fear is certainly not personal," replied the other proudly; "of that your Highness may rest well assured."

"I had supposed as much," returned the Prince, with undisturbed good humour; "but I was unwilling to remind you of the difference in our stations. No more—no more," he added, seeing Geraldine about to apologize, "you stand excused."

And he smoked placidly, leaning against a railing, until the young man returned.

"Well," he asked, 'has our reception been arranged?"

"Follow me," was the reply. "The President will see you in the cabinet. And let me warn you to be frank in your answers. I have stood your guarantee; but the Club requires a searching inquiry before admission; for the indiscretion of a single member would lead to the dispersion of the whole society for ever."

The Prince and Geraldine put their heads together for a moment. "Bear me out in this," said the one; and "bear me out in that," said the other; and by boldly taking up the characters of men with whom both were acquainted, they had come to an agreement in a twinkling, and were ready to follow their guide into the President's cabinet.

There were no formidable obstacles to pass. The outer door stood open; the door of the cabinet was ajar; and there, in a small but very high apartment, the young man left them once more.

"He will be here immediately," he said, with a nod, as he disappeared.

Voices were audible in the cabinet through the folding doors which formed one end; and now and then the noise of a champagne cork, followed by a burst of laughter, intervened among the sounds of conversation. A single tall window looked out upon the river and the embankment; and by the disposition of the lights they judged themselves not far from Charing Cross station. The furniture was scanty, and the coverings worn to the thread; and there was nothing movable except a hand-bell in the centre of a round table, and the hats and coats of a considerable party hung round the wall on pegs.

"What sort of á den is this?" said Geraldine.

"That is what I have come to see," replied the Prince.

"If they keep live devils on the premises, the thing may grow amusing."

Just then the folding door was opened no more than was necessary for the passage of a human body; and there entered at the same moment a louder buzz of talk, and the redoubtable President of the Suicide Club. The President was a man of fifty or upwards; large and rambling in his gait, with shaggy side whiskers, a bald top to his head, and a veiled grey eye, which now and then emitted a twinkle. His mouth, which embraced a large cigar, he kept continually screwing round and round and from side to side, as he looked sagaciously and coldly at the strangers. He was dressed in light tweeds, with his neck very open in a striped shirt collar; and carried a minute book under one arm.

"Good evening," said he, after he had closed the door behind him. "I am told you wish to speak with me."

"We have a desire, sir, to join the Suicide Club," replied the Colonel.

The President rolled his cigar about in his mouth.

"What is that?" he said abruptly.

"Pardon me," returned the Colonel "but I believe you are the person best qualified to give us information on that point."

"I?" cried the President. "A Suicide Club? Come, come! this is a frolic for All Fools' Day. I can make allowances for gentlemen who get merry in their liquor; but let there be an end to this."

"Call your Club what you will," said the Colonel, "you have some company behind these doors, and we insist on joining it."

"Sir," returned the President curtly, "you have made a mistake. This is a private house, and you must leave it instantly."

The Prince had remained quietly in his seat throughout this little colloquy; but now, when the Colonel looked over to him as much as to say, "Take your answer and come away, for God's sake!" he drew his cheroot from his mouth, and spoke:

"I have come here," said he, "upon the invitation of a friend of yours. He has doubtless informed you of my intention in thus intruding on your party. Let me remind you that a person in my circumstances has exceedingly little to bind him, and is not at all likely to tolerate much rudeness. I am a very quiet man, as a usual thing; but, my dear sir, you are either going to oblige me in the little matter of which you are aware, or you shall very bitterly repent that you ever admitted me to your antechamber."

The President laughed aloud.

"That is the way to speak," said he. "You are a man who is a man. You know the way to my heart, and can do what you like with me—Will you," he continued, addressing Geraldine, "will you step aside for a few minutes? I shall finish first with your companion, and some of the Club's formalities require to be fulfilled in private."

With these words he opened the door of a small closet, into which he shut the Colonel.

"I believe in you," he said to Florizel, as soon as they were alone; "but are you sure of your friend?"

"Not so sure as I am of myself, though he has more cogent reasons," answered Florizel, "but sure enough to bring him here without alarm. He has had enough to cure the most tenacious man of life. He was cashiered the other day for cheating at cards.

"A good reason, I dare say," replied the President; "at least, we have another in the same case, and I feel sure of him. Have you also been in the Service, may I ask?"

"I have," was the reply; "but I was too lazy, I left it early."

"What is your reasons for being tired of life?" pursued the President.

"The same, as near as I can make out," answered the Prince; "unadulterated laziness."

The President started. "D—n it," said he, "you must have something better than that."

"I have no more money," added Florizel. "That is also a vexation, without doubt. It brings my sense of idleness to an acute point."

The President rolled his cigar round in his mouth for some seconds, directing his gaze straight into the eyes of this unusual neophyte; but the Prince supported his scrutiny with unabashed good temper.

"If I had not a deal of experience," said the President at last, "I should turn you off. But I know the world; and this much anyway, that the most frivolous excuses for a suicide are often the toughest to stand by. And when I downright like a man, as I do you, sir, I would rather strain the regulation than deny him."

The Prince and the Colonel, one after the other, were subjected to a long and particular interrogatory: the Prince alone; but Geraldine in the presence of the Prince, so that the President might observe the countenance of the one while the other was being warmly cross-examined. The result was satisfactory; and the President, after having booked a few details of each case, produced a form of oath to be accepted. Nothing could be conceived more passive than the obedience promised, or more stringent than the terms by which the juror bound himself. The man who forfeited a pledge so awful could scarcely have a rag of honour or any of the consolations of religion left to him. Florizel signed the document, but not without a shudder; the Colonel followed his example with an air of great depression. Then the President received the entry money; and without more ado, introduced the two friends into the smoking-room of the Suicide Club.

The smoking-room of the Suicide Club was the same height as the cabinet into which it opened, but much larger, and papered from top to bottom with an imitation of oak wainscot. A large and cheerful fire and a number of gas-jets illuminated the company. The Prince and his follower made the number up to eighteen. Most of the party were smoking and drinking champagne; a feverish hilarity reigned, with sudden and rather ghastly pauses.

"Is this a full meeting?" asked the Prince.

"Middling," said the President. "By the way," he added, "if you have any money, it is usual to offer some champagne. It keeps up a good spirit, and is one of my own little perquisites."

"Hammersmith," said Florizel, "I may leave the champagne to you."

And with that he turned away and began to go round among the guests. Accustomed to play the host in the highest circles, he charmed and dominated all whom he approached; there was something at once winning and authoritative in his address; and his extraordinary coolness gave him yet another distinction in this half-maniacal society. As he went from one to another he kept both his eyes and ears open, and soon began to gain a general idea of the people among whom he found himself. As in all other places of resort, one type predominated: people in the prime of youth, with every show of intelligence and sensibility in their appearance, but with little promise of strength or the quality that makes success. Few were much above thirty and not a few were still in their teens. They stood, leaning on tables and shifting their feet; sometimes they smoked extraordinarily fast, and sometimes they let their cigars go out; some talked well, but the conversation of others was plainly the result of nervous tension, and was equally without wit or purport. As each new bottle of champagne was opened, there was a manifest improvement in gaiety. Only two were seated—one in a chair in the recess of the window with his head hanging and his hands plunged deep into his trousers pockets, pale, visibly moist with perspiration, saying never a word, a very wreck of soul and body; the other sat on the divan close by the chimney, and attracted notice by a trenchant dissimilarity from all the rest. He was probably upwards of forty, but he looked fully ten years older; and Florizel thought he had never seen a man more naturally hideous, nor one more ravaged by disease and ruinous excitements. He was no more than skin and bone, was partly paralysed, and wore spectacles of such unusual power, that his eyes appeared through the glasses greatly magnified and distorted in shape. Except the Prince and the President, he was the only person in the room who preserved the composure of ordinary life.

There was little decency among the members of the Club. Some boasted of the disgraceful actions, the consequences of which had reduced them to seek refuge in death; and the others listened without disapproval. There was a tacit understanding against moral judgements; and whoever passed the Club doors enjoyed already some of the immunities of the tomb. They drank to each other's memories, and to those of notable suicides in the past. They compared and developed their different views of death—some declaring that it was no more than blackness and cessation; others full of hope that that very night they should be scaling the stars and commercing with the mighty dead.

"To the eternal memory of Baron Trenck, the type of suicides!" cried one. "He went out of a small cell into a smaller, that he might come forth again to freedom."

"For my part," said a second, "I wish no more than a bandage for my eyes and cotton for my ears. Only they have no cotton thick enough in this world."

A third was for reading the mysteries of life in a future state; and a fourth professed that he would never have joined the Club if he had not been induced to believe in Mr Darwin.

"I could not bear," said this remarkable suicide, "to be descended from an ape."

Altogether the Prince was disappointed by the bearing and conversation of the members.

"It does not seem to me," he thought, "a matter for so much disturbance. If a man has made up his mind to kill himself, let him do it, in God's name, like a gentleman. This flutter and big talk is out of place."

In the meanwhile Colonel Geraldine was a prey to the blackest apprehensions; the Club and its rules were still a mystery, and he looked round the room for someone who should be able to set his mind at rest. In his survey his eye lighted on the paralytic person with the strong spectacles; and seeing him so exceedingly tranquil, he besought the President, who was going in and out of the room under a pressure of business, to present him to the gentleman on the divan.

The functionary explained the needlessness of all such formalities within the Club, but nevertheless presented Mr Hammersmith to Mr Malthus.

Mr Malthus looked at the colonel curiously, and then requested him to take a seat upon his right.

"You are a new-comer," he said, "and wish information? You have come to the proper source. It is two years since I first visited this charming Club."

The Colonel breathed again. If Mr Malthus had frequented the place for two years there could be little danger for the Prince in a single evening. But Geraldine was none the less astonished, and began to suspect a mystification.

"What!" cried he, "two years! I thought—but indeed I see I have been made the subject of a pleasantry."

"By no means," replied Mr Malthus mildly. "My case is peculiar. I am not, properly speaking, a suicide at all; but, as it were, an honorary member. I rarely visit the Club twice in two months. My infirmity and the kindness of the President have procured me these little immunities, for which besides I pay at an advanced rate. Even as it is my luck has been extraordinary."

"I am afraid," said the Colonel, "that I must ask you to be more explicit. You must remember that I am still most imperfectly acquainted with the rules of the Club."

"An ordinary member who comes here in search of death like yourself," replied the paralytic, "returns every evening until fortune favours him. He can even, if he is penniless, get board and lodging room the President: very fair, I believe, and clean, although, of course, not luxurious; that could hardly be, considering the exiguity (if I may so express myself) of the subscription. And then the President's company is a delicacy in itself."

"Indeed!" cried Geraldine, "he had not greatly prepossessed me."

"Ah!" said Mr Malthus, "you do not know the man: the drollest fellow! What stories! What cynicism! He knows life to admiration, and between ourselves, is probably the most corrupt rogue in Christendom."

"And he also," asked the Colonel, "is a permanency—like yourself, if I may say so without offence?"

"Indeed, he is a permanency in a very different sense from me," replied Mr Malthus. "I have been graciously spared, but I must go at last. Now he never plays. He shuffles and deals for the Club, and makes the necessary arrangements. That man, my dear Mr Hammersmith, is the very soul of ingenuity. For three years he has pursued in London his useful, and, I think I may add, his artistic calling; and not so much as a whisper of suspicion has been once aroused. I believe him myself to be inspired. You doubtless remember the celebrated case, six months ago, of the gentleman who was accidentally poisoned in a chemist's shop? That was one of the least rich, one of the least racy, of his notions; but then, how simple! and how safe!"

"You astound me," said the Colonel. "Was that unfortunate gentleman one of the—" He was about to say "victims"; but bethinking himself in time, he substituted—"members of the Club?" In the same flash of thought it occurred to him that Mr Malthus himself had not at all spoken in the tone of one who is in love with death; and he added hurriedly:

"But I perceive I am still in the dark. You speak of shuffling and dealing; pray for what end? And since you seem rather unwilling to die than otherwise, I must own that I cannot conceave what brings you here at all."

"You say truly that you are in the dark," replied Mr Malthus with more animation. "Why, my dear sir, this Club is the temple of intoxication. If my enfeebled health could support the excitement more often, you may depend upon it I should be more often here. It requires all the sense of duty engendered by a long habit of ill-health and careful regimen, to keep me from excess in this, which is, I may say, my last dissipation. I have tried them all, sir," he went on, laying his hand on Geraldine's arm, "all without exception, and I declare to you, upon my honour, there is not one of them that has not been grossly and untruthfully over-rated. People trifle with love. Now, I deny that love is a strong passion. Fear is the strong passion; it is with fear that you must trifle, if you wish to taste the intensest joys of living. Envy me—envy me, sir," he added with a chuckle, "I am a coward!"

Geraldine could scarcely repress a movement of repulsion for this deplorable wretch; but he commanded himself with an effort, and continued his inquiries.

"How, sir," he asked, "is the excitement so artfully prolonged? and where is there any element of uncertainty?"

"I must tell you how the victim for every evening is selected," returned Mr Malthus; "and not only the victim, but another member, who is to be the instrument in the Club's hands, and death's high priest for that occasion."

"Good God!" said the Colonel, "do they then kill each other?"

"The trouble of suicide is removed in that way," returned Malthus with a nod.

"Merciful Heavens!" ejaculated the Colonel "and may you—may I—may the—my friend I mean—may any of us be pitched upon this evening as the slayer of another man's body and immortal spirit? Can such things be possible among men born of women? Oh! infamy of infamies!"

He was about to rise in his horror, when he caught the Prince's eye. It was fixed upon him from across the room with a frowning and angry stare. And in a moment Geraldine recovered his composure.

"After all," he added, "why not? And since you say the game is interesting, *vogue la galère*—I follow the Club!"

Mr Malthus had keenly enjoyed the Colonel's amazement and disgust. He had the vanity of wickedness; and it pleased him to see another man give way to a generous movement, while he felt himself, in his entire corruption, superior to such emotions.

"You now, after your first moment of surprise," said he, "are in a position to appreciate the delights of our society. You can see how it combines the excitement of a gaming-table, a duel, and a Roman amphitheatre. The Pagans did well enough; I cordially admire the refinement of their minds; but it has been reserved for a Christian country to attain this extreme, this quintessence, this absolute of poignancy. You will understand how vapid are all amusements to a man who has acquired a taste for this one. The game we play," he continued, "is one of extreme simplicity. A full pack—but I perceive you are about to see the thing in progress. Will you lend me the help of your arm? I am unfortunately paralysed."

Indeed, just as Mr Malthus was beginning his description, another pair of folding-doors was thrown open, and the whole Club began to pass, not without some hurry, into the adjoining room. It was similar in every respect to the one from which it was entered, but somewhat differently furnished. The centre was occupied by a long green table, at which the President sat shuffling a pack of cards with great particularity. Even with the stick and the Colonel's arm, Mr Malthus walked with so much difficulty that everyone was seated before this pair and the Prince, who had waited for them, entered the apartment; and in consequence, the three took seats close together at the lower end of the board.

"It is a pack of fifty-two," whispered Mr Malthus. "Watch for the ace of spades, which is the sign of death, and the ace of clubs, which designates the official of the night. Happy, happy young men!" he added. "You have good eyes, and can follow the game. Alas! I cannot tell an ace from a deuce across the table."

And he proceeded to equip himself with a second pair of spectacles.

"I must at least watch the faces," he explained.

The Colonel rapidly informed his friend of all that he had learned from the honorary member, and of the horrible alternative that lay before them. The Prince was conscious of a deadly chill and a contraction about his heart; he swallowed with difficulty, and looked from side to side like a man in a maze.

"One bold stroke," whispered the Colonel, "and we may still escape."

But the suggestion recalled the Prince's spirits.

"Silence!" said he. "Let me see that you can play like a gentleman for any stake, however serious."

And he looked about him, once more to all appearance at his ease, although his heart beat quickly, and he was conscious of an unpleasant heat in his bosom. The members were all very quiet and intent; everyone was pale, but none so pale as Mr Malthus. His eyes protruded; his head kept nodding involuntarily upon his spine; his hands found their way, one after the other, to his mouth, where they made clutches at his tremulous and ashen lips. It was plain that the honorary member enjoyed his membership on very startling terms.

"Attention, gentlemen!" said the President.

And he began slowly dealing the cards about the table in the reverse direction, pausing until each man had shown his card. Nearly everyone hesitated; and sometimes you would see a player's fingers stumble more than once before he could turn over the momentous slip of pasteboard. As the Prince's turn drew nearer, he was conscious of a growing and almost suffocating excitement; but he had somewhat of the gambler's nature, and recognized almost with astonishment that there was a degree of pleasure in his sensations. The nine of clubs fell to his lot; the three of spades was dealt to Geraldine; and the queen of hearts to Mr Malthus, who was unable to suppress a sob of relief. The young man of the cream tarts almost immediately afterwards turned over the ace of clubs, and remained frozen with horror, the card still resting on his finger; he had not come there to kill, but to be killed; and the Prince in his generous sympathy with his position almost forgot the peril that still hung over himself and his friend.

The deal was coming round again, and still Death's card had not come out. The players held their respiration, and only breathed by gasps. The Prince received another club; Geraldine had a diamond; but when Mr Malthus turned up his card a horrible noise, like that of something breaking, issued from his mouth; and he rose from his seat and sat down again, with no sign of his paralysis. It was the ace of spades. The honorary member had trifled once too often with his terrors.

Conversation broke out again almost at once. The players relaxed their rigid attitudes, and began to rise from the table and stroll back by twos and threes into the smoking-room. The President stretched his arms and yawned, like a man who has finished his day's work. But Mr Malthus sat in his place, with his head in his hands, and his hands upon the table, drunk and motionless—a thing stricken down.

The Prince and Geraldine made their escape at once. In the cold night air their horror of what they had witnessed was redoubled.

"Alas!" cried the Prince, "to be bound by an oath in

such a matter! to allow this wholesale trade in murder to be continued with profit and impunity! If I but dared to forfeit my pledge!"

"That is impossible of your Highness," replied the Colonel, "whose honour is the honour of Bohemia. But I dare, and may with propriety, forfeit mine."

"Geraldine," said the Prince, "if your honour suffers in any of the adventures into which you follow me, not only will I never pardon you, but—what I believe will much more sensibly affect you—I should never forgive myself."

"I receive your Highness's commands," replied the Colonel. "Shall we go from this accursed spot?"

"Yes," said the Prince. "Call a cab in Heaven's name, and let me try to forget in slumber the memory of this night's disgrace." But it was notable that he carefully read the name of the court before he left it.

The next morning, as soon as the Prince was stirring, Colonel Geraldine brought him a daily newspaper, with the following paragraph marked:

'MELANCHOLY ACCIDENT.—This morning, about two o'clock, Mr Bartholomew Malthus, of 16 Chepstow Place, Westbourne Grove, on his way home from a party at a friend's house, fell over the upper parapet in Trafalgar Square, fracturing his skull and breaking a leg and an arm. Death was instantaneous. Mr Malthus, accompanied by a friend, was engaged in looking for a cab at the time of the unfortunate occurrence. As Mr Malthus was paralytic, it is thought that his fall may have been occasioned by another seizure. The unhappy gentleman was well known in the most respectable circles, and his loss will be widely and deeply deplored.'

"If ever a soul went straight to hell," said Geraldine solemnly, "it was that paralytic man's."

The Prince buried his face in his hands and remained silent.

"I am almost rejoiced," continued the Colonel, "to know that he is dead. But for our young man of the cream tarts I confess my heart bleeds."

"Geraldine," said the Prince, raising his face, "that unhappy lad was last night as innocent as you and I, and this morning the guilt of blood is on his soul. When I think of the President, my heart grows sick within me. I do not know how it shall be done, but I shall have that scoundrel at my mercy as there is a God in Heaven. What an experience, what a lesson, was that game of cards!"

"One," said the Colonel, "never to be repeated."

The Prince remained so long without replying that Geraldine grew alarmed.

"You cannot mean to return," he said. "You have suffered too much and seen too much horror already. The duties of your high position forbid the repetition of the hazard."

"There is much in what you say," replied Prince Florizel, "and I am not altogether pleased with my own determination. Alas! in the clothes of the greatest potentate, what is there but a man? I never felt my weakness more acutely than now, Geraldine, but it is stronger than I. Can I cease to interest myself in the fortunes of the unhappy young man who supped with us some hours ago? Can I leave the President to follow his nefarious career unwatched? Can I begin an adventure so entrancing, and not follow it to an end? No, Geraldine: you ask of the Prince more than the man is able to perform. Tonight, once more, we take our places at the table of the Suicide Club."

Colonel Geraldine fell upon his knees.

"Will your Highness take my life?" he cried. "It is his—his freely; but do not, oh do not! let him ask me to countenance so terrible a risk."

"Colonel Geraldine," replied the Prince, with some haughtiness of manner, "your life is absolutely your own. I only looked for obedience; and when that is unwillingly rendered, I shall look for that no longer. I add one word: your importunity in this affair has been sufficient."

The Master of the Horse regained his feet at once.

"Your Highness," he said, "may I be excused in my attendance this afternoon? I dare not, as an honourable man, venture a second time into that fatal house until I have perfectly ordered my affairs. Your Highness shall meet, I promise him, with no more opposition from the most devoted and grateful of his servants."

"My dear Geraldine," returned Prince Florizel, "I always regret when you oblige me to remember my rank. Dispose of your day as you think fit, but be here before eleven in the same disguise."

The Club, on this second evening, was not so fully attended; and when Geraldine and the Prince arrived, there were not above half a dozen persons in the smoking-room. His Highness took the President aside and congratulated him warmly on the demise of Mr Malthus.

"I like," he said, "to meet with capacity, and certainly find much of it in you. Your profession is of a very delicate nature, but I see you are well qualified to conduct it with success and secrecy."

The President was somewhat affected by these compliments from one of his Highness's superior bearing. He acknowledged them almost with humility.

"Poor Malthy!" he added, "I shall hardly know the Club without him. The most of my patrons are boys, sir, and poetical boys, who are not much company for me. Not but what Malthy had some poetry, too; but it was of a kind that I could understand."

"I can readily imagine you should find yourself in sympathy with Mr Malthus," returned the Prince. "He struck me as a man of a very original disposition."

The young man of the cream tarts was in the room, but painfully depressed and silent. His late companions sought in vain to lead him into conversation.

"How bitterly I wish," he cried, "that I had never brought you to this infamous abode! Begone, while you are clean-handed. If you could have heard the old man scream as he fell, and the noise of his bones upon the pavement! Wish me, if you have any kindness to so fallen a being—wish the ace of spades for me tonight!"

A few more members dropped in as the evening went on, but the Club did not muster more than the devil's dozen when they took their places at the table. The Prince was again conscious of a certain joy in his alarms; but he was astonished to see Geraldine so much more self-possessed than on the night before.

"It is extraordinary," thought the Prince, "that a will, made or unmade, should so greatly influence a young man's spirit."

"Attention, gentlemen!" said the President, and he began to deal.

Three times the cards went all round the table, and neither of the marked cards had yet fallen from his hand. The excitement as he began the fourth distribution was overwhelming. There were just cards enough to go once more entirely round. The Prince, who sat second from the dealer's left, would receive, in the reverse mode of dealing practised at the Club, the second last card. The third player turned up a black ace—it was the ace of clubs. The next received a diamond, the next a heart, and so on; but the ace of spades was still undelivered. At last, Geraldine, who sat upon the Prince's left, turned his card; it was an ace, but the ace of hearts.

When Prince Florizel saw his fate upon the table in front of him, his heart stood still. He was a brave man, but the sweat poured off his face. There were exactly fifty chances out of a hundred that he was doomed. He reversed the card; it was the ace of spades. A loud roaring filled his brain, and the table swam before his eyes. He heard the player on his right break into a fit of laughter that sounded between mirth and disappointment; he saw the company rapidly dispersing, but his mind was full of other thoughts. He recognized how foolish, how criminal, had been his conduct. In perfect health, in the prime of his years, the heir to a throne, he had gambled away his future and that of a brave and loyal country. "God," he cried, "God forgive me!" And with that, the confusion of his senses passed away, and he regained his self-possession in a moment.

To his surprise Geraldine had disappeared. There was no one in the card-room but his destined butcher consulting with the President, and the young man of the cream tarts, who slipped up to the Prince and whispered in his ear:

"I would give a million, if I had it, for your luck."

His Highness could not help reflecting, as the young man departed, that he would have sold his opportunity for a much more moderate sum.

The whispered conference now came to an end. The holder of the ace of clubs left the room with a look of intelligence, and the President, approaching the unfortunate Prince, proffered him his hand.

"I am pleased to have met you, sir," said he, "and pleased to have been in a position to do you this trifling service. At least, you cannot complain of delay. On the second evening—what a stroke of luck!"

The Prince endeavoured in vain to articulate something in response, but his mouth was dry and his tongue seemed paralysed.

"You feel a little sickish?" asked the President, with some show of solicitude. "Most gentlemen do. Will you take a little brandy?"

The Prince signified in the affirmative, and the other immediately filled some of the spirit into a tumbler.

"Poor old Malthy!" ejaculated the President, as the Prince drained the glass. "He drank near upon a pint, and little enough good it seemed to do him!"

"I am more amenable to treatment," said the Prince, a good deal revived. "I am my own man again at once, as you perceive. And so, let me ask you, what are my directions?"

"You will proceed along the Strand in the direction of the City, and on the left-hand pavement, until you meet the gentleman who has just left the room. He will continue your instructions, and him you will have the kindness to obey; the authority of the Club is vested in his person for the night. And now," added the President, "I wish you a pleasant walk."

Florizel acknowledged the salutation rather awkwardly, and took his leave. He passed through the smoking-room, where the bulk of the players were still consuming champagne, some of which he had himself ordered and paid for; and he was surprised to find himself cursing them in his heart. He put on his hat and greatcoat in the cabinet, and selected his umbrella from a corner. The familiarity of these acts, and the thought that he was about them for the last time, betrayed him into a fit of laughter which sounded unpleasantly in his own ears. He conceived a reluctance to leave the cabinet, and turned instead to the window. The sight of the lamps and the darkness recalled him to himself.

"Come, come, I must be a man," he thought, "and tear myself away."

At the corner of Box Court three men fell upon Prince Florizel, and he was unceremoniously thrust into a carriage, which at once drove rapidly away. There was already an occupant.

"Will your Highness pardon my zeal?" said a well-known voice.

The Prince threw himself upon the Colonel's neck in a passion of relief.

"How can I ever thank you?" he cried. "And how was this effected?"

Although he had been willing to march upon his doom, he was overjoyed to yield to friendly violence, and return once more to life and hope.

"You can thank me effectually enough," replied the Colonel, "by avoiding all such dangers in the future. And as for your second question, all has been managed by the simplest means. I arranged this afternoon with a celebrated detective. Secrecy has been promised and paid for. Your own servants have been principally engaged in the affair. The house in Box Court has been surrounded since nightfall, and this, which is one of your own carriages, has been awaiting you for nearly an hour."

"And the miserable creature who was to have slain me—what of him?" inquired the Prince.

"He was pinioned as he left the Club," replied the Colonel, "and now awaits your sentence at the Palace, where he will soon be joined by his accomplices."

"Geraldine," said the Prince, "you have saved me against my explicit orders, and you have done well. I owe you not only my life, but a lesson; and I should be unworthy of my rank if I did not show myself grateful to my teacher. Let it be yours to choose the manner."

There was a pause, during which the carriage continued to speed through the streets, and the two men were each buried in his own reflections. The silence was broken by Colonel Geraldine.

"Your Highness," said he, "has by this time a considerable body of prisoners. There is at least one criminal among the number to whom justice should be dealt. Our oath forbids us all recourse to law; and discretion would forbid it equally if the oath were loosened. May I inquire your Highness's intention?"

"It is decided," answered Florizel; "the President must fall in duel. It only remains to choose his adversary."

"Your Highness has permitted me to name my own recompense," said the Colonel. "Will he permit me to ask the appointment of my brother? It is an honourable post, but I dare assure your Highness that the lad will acquit himself with credit."

"You ask me an ungracious favour," said the Prince, "but I must refuse you nothing."

The Colonel kissed his hand with the greatest affection; and at that moment the carriage rolled under the archway of the Prince's splendid residence.

An hour after, Florizel in his official robes, and covered with all the orders of Bohemia, received the members of the Suicide Club.

"Foolish and wicked men," said he, "as many of you as have been driven into this strait by the lack of fortune shall receive employment and remuneration from my officers. Those who suffer under a sense of guilt must have recourse to a higher and more generous Potentate than I. I feel pity for all of you, deeper than you can imagine; tomorrow you shall tell me your stories; and as you answer more frankly, I shall be the more able to remedy your misfortunes. As for you," he added, turning to the President, "I should only offend a person of your parts by any offer of assistance; but I have instead a piece of diversion to propose to you. Here," laying his hand on the shoulder of Colonel Geraldine's young brother, "is an officer of mine who desires to make a little tour upon the Continent: and I ask you, as a favour, to accompany him on this excursion. Do you," he went on, changing his tone, "do you shoot well with the pistol? Because you may have need of that accomplishment. When two men go travelling together, it is best to be prepared for all. Let me add that, if by any chance you should lose young Mr Geraldine upon the way, I shall always have another member of my household to place at your disposal; and I am known, Mr President, to have long eyesight and as long an arm."

With these words, said with much sternness, the Prince concluded his address. Next morning the members of the Club were suitably provided for by his munificence, and the President set forth upon his travels, under the supervision of Mr Geraldine, and a pair of faithful and adroit lackeys, well trained in the Prince's household. Not content with this, discreet agents were put in possession of the house in Box Court, and all letters or visitors for the Suicide Club or its officials were to be examined by Prince Florizel in person.

Here (says my Arabian author) *ends the* STORY OF THE YOUNG MAN WITH THE CREAM TARTS, *who is now a comfortable householder in Wigmore Street, Cavendish Square. The number, for obvious reasons, I suppress. Those who care to pursue the adventures of Prince Florizel and the President of the Suicide Club may read the* HISTORY OF THE PHYSICIAN AND THE SARATOGA TRUNK.

2

Story of the Physician and the Saratoga Trunk

Mr Silas Q. Scuddamore was a young American of a simple and harmless disposition, which was the more to his credit as he came from New England—a quarter of the New World not precisely famous for those qualities. Although he was exceedingly rich, he kept a note of all his expenses in a little paper pocket-book; and he had chosen to study the attractions of Paris from the seventh story of what is called a furnished hotel, in the Latin Quarter. There was a great deal of habit in his penuriousness; and his virtue, which was very remarkable among his associates, was principally founded upon diffidence and youth.

The next room to his was inhabited by a lady, very attractive in her air and very elegant in toilette, whom, on his first arrival he had taken for a countess. In course of time he had learned that, she was known by the name of Madame Zéphyrine, and that whatever station she occupied in life it was not that of a person of title. Madame Zéphyrine, probably in the hope of enchanting the young American, used to flaunt by him on the stairs with a civil inclination, a word of course, and a knock-down look out of her black eyes, and disappear in a rustle of silk, and with the revelation of an admirable foot and ankle. But these advances, so far from encouraging Mr Scuddamore, plunged him into the depths of depression and bashfulness. She had come to him several times for a light, or to apologize for the imaginary depredations of her poodle; but his mouth was closed in the presence of so superior a being, his French promptly left him, and he could only stare and stammer until she was gone. The slenderness of their intercourse did not prevent him from throwing out insinuations of a very glorious order when he was safely alone with a few males.

The room on the other side of the American's—for there were three rooms on a floor in the hotel—was tenanted by an old English physician of rather doubtful reputation. Dr Noel, for that was his name, had been forced to leave London, where he enjoyed a large and increasing practice; and it was hinted that the police had been the instigators of this change of scene. At least he, who had made something of a figure in earlier life, now dwelt in the Latin Quarter in great simplicity and solitude, and devoted much of his time to study. Mr Scuddamore had made his acquaintance, and the pair would now and then dine together frugally in a restaurant across the street.

Silas Q. Scuddamore had many little vices of the more respectable order, and was not restrained by delicacy from indulging them in many rather doubtful ways. Chief among his foibles stood curiosity. He was a born gossip; and life, and especially those parts of it in which he had no experience, interested him to the degree of passion. He was a pert, invincible questioner, pushing his inquiries with equal pertinacity and indiscretion: he had been observed, when he took a letter to the post, to weigh it in his hand, to turn it over and over, and to study the address with care; and when he found a flaw in the partition between his room and Madame Zéphyrine's, instead of filling it up, made use of it as a spy-hole on his neighbour's affairs.

One day, in the end of March, his curiosity growing as it was indulged, he enlarged the hole a little further, so that he might command another corner of the room. That evening, when he went as usual to inspect Madame Zéphyrine's movements, he was astonished to find the aperture obscured in an odd manner on the other side, and still more abashed when the obstacle was suddenly withdrawn and a titter of laughter reached his ears. Some of the plaster had evidently betrayed the secret of his spy hole, and his neighbour had been returning the compliment in kind. Mr Scuddamore was moved to a very acute feeling of annoyance; he condemned Madame Zéphyrine unmercifully; he even blamed himself; but when he found, next day, that she had taken no means to baulk him of his favourite pastime, he continued to profit by her carelessness, and gratify his idle curiosity.

The next day Madame Zéphyrine received a long visit from a tall, loosely built man of fifty or upwards, whom Silas had not hitherto seen. His tweed suit and coloured shirt, no less than his shaggy sidewhiskers, identified him as a Britisher, and his dull grey eye affected Silas with a sense of cold. He kept screwing his mouth from side to side and round and round during the whole colloquy, which was carried on in whispers. More than once it seemed to the young New Englander as if their gestures indicated his own apartment; but the only thing definite he could gather by the most scrupulous attention was this remark made by the Englishman in a somewhat higher key, as if in answer to some reluctance or opposition:

"I have studied his taste to a nicety, and I tell you again and again you are the only woman of the sort that I can lay my hands on."

In answer to this, Madame Zéphyrine sighed, and appeared by a gesture to resign herself, like one yielding to unqualified authority. That afternoon the observatory was finally blinded, a wardrobe having been drawn in front of it upon the other side; and while Silas was still lamenting over this misfortune, which he attributed to the Britisher's malign suggestion, the concierge brought him up a letter in a female handwriting. It was conceived in French of no very rigorous orthography, bore no signature, and in the most encouraging terms invited the young American to be present in a certain part of the Bullier Ball at eleven o'clock that night. Curiosity and timidity fought a long battle in his heart; sometimes he was all virtue, sometimes all fire and daring; and the result of it was that, long before ten, Mr Silas Q. Scuddamore presented himself in unimpeachable attire at the door of the Bullier Ball Rooms and paid his entry money with a sense of reckless devilry that was not without its charm.

It was Carnival time, and the Ball was very full and noisy. The lights and the crowd at first rather abashed our young adventurer, and then, mounting to his brain with a sort of intoxication, put him in possession of more than his own share of manhood. He felt ready to face the devil, and strutted in the ballroom with the swagger of a cavalier. While he was thus parading he became aware of Madame Zéphyrine and her Britisher in conference behind a pillar. The catlike spirit of eavesdropping overcame him at once. He stole nearer and nearer on the couple from behind until he was within earshot.

"That is the man," the Britisher was saying; "there—with the long blond hair—speaking to a girl in green."

Silas identified a very handsome young fellow of small stature, who was plainly the object of this designation.

"It is well," said Madame Zéphyrine. "I shall do my utmost. But, remember, the best of us may fail in such a matter."

"Tut!" returned her companion; "I answer for the result. Have I not chosen you from thirty? Go; but be wary of the Prince. I cannot think what cursed accident has brought him here tonight. As if there were not a dozen balls in Paris better worth his notice than this riot of students and counter-jumpers! See him where he sits, more like a reigning Emperor at home than a Prince upon his holidays."

Silas was again lucky. He observed a person of rather a full build, strikingly handsome, and of a very stately and courteous demeanour, seated at table with another handsome young man, several years his junior, who addressed him with conspicuous deference. The name of Prince struck gratefully on Silas's Republican hearing, and the aspect of the person to whom that name was applied exercised its usual charm upon his mind. He left Madame Zéphyrine and her Englishman to take care of each other, and threading his way through the assembly, approached the table which the Prince and his confidant had honoured with their choice.

"I tell you, Geraldine," the former was saying, "the

action is madness. Yourself (I am glad to remember it) chose your brother for this perilous service, and you are bound in duty to have a guard upon his conduct. He had consented to delay so many days in Paris; that was already an imprudence, considering the character of the mall he has to deal with; but now, when he is within eight-and-forty hours of his departure, when he is within two or three days of the decisive trial, I ask you, is this a place for him to spend his time? He should be in a gallery at practice; he should be sleeping long hours and taking moderate exercise on foot; he should be on a rigorous diet, without white wines or brandy. Does the dog imagine we are all playing comedy? The thing is deadly earnest, Geraldine."

"I know the lad too well to interfere," replied Colonel Geraldine, "and well enough not to be alarmed. He is more cautious than you fancy, and of an indomitable spirit. If it had been a woman I should not say so much, but I trust the President to him and the two valets without an instant's apprehension."

"I am gratified to hear you say so," replied the Prince, "but my mind is not at rest. These servants are well-trained spies, and already has not this miscreant succeeded three times in eluding their observation and spending several hours on end in private, and most likely dangerous affairs? An amateur might have lost him by accident, but if Rudolph and Jerome were thrown off the scent, it must have been done on purpose, and by a man who had a cogent reason and exceptional resources."

"I believe the question is now one between my brother and myself," replied Geraldine, with a shade of offence in his tone.

"I permit it to be so, Colonel Geraldine," returned Prince Florizel. "Perhaps, for that very reason, you should be all the more ready to accept my counsels. But enough. That girl in yellow dances well."

And the talk veered into the ordinary topics of a Paris ballroom in the Carnival.

Silas remembered where he was, and that the hour was already near at hand when he ought to be upon the scene of his assignation. The more he reflected the less he liked the prospect, and as at that moment an eddy in the crowd began to draw him in the direction of the door, he suffered it to carry him away without resistance. The eddy stranded him in a corner under the gallery, where his ear was immediately struck with the voice of Madame Zéphyrine. She was speaking in French with the young man of the blond locks who had been pointed out by the strange Britisher not half an hour before.

"I have a character at stake," she said, "or I would put no other condition than my heart recommends. But you have only to say so much to the porter, and he will let you go by without a word."

"But why this talk of debt?" objected her companion.

"Heavens!" said she, "do you think I do not understand my own hotel?" And she went by, clinging affectionately to her companion's arm.

This put Silas in mind of his billet.

"Ten minutes hence," thought he, "and I may be walking with as beautiful a woman as that, and even better dressed—perhaps a real lady, possibly a woman of title."

And then he remembered the spelling, and was a little downcast.

"But it may have been written by her maid," he imagined.

The clock was only a few minutes from the hour, and this immediate proximity set his heart beating at a curious and rather disagreeable speed. He reflected with relief that he was in no way bound to put in an appearance. Virtue and cowardice were together, and he made once more for the door, but this time of his own accord, and battling against the stream of people which was now moving in a contrary direction. Perhaps this prolonged resistance wearied him, or perhaps he was in that frame of mind when merely to continue in the same determination for a certain number of minutes produces a reaction and a different purpose. Certainly, at least, he wheeled about for a third time, and did not stop until he had found a place of concealment within a few yards of the appointed place.

He went through an agony of spirit, in which he several times prayed to God for help, for Silas had been devoutly educated. He had now not the least inclination for the meeting; nothing kept him from flight but a silly fear lest he should be thought unmanly; but this was so powerful that it kept head against all other motives; and although it could not decide him to advance, prevented him from definitely running away. At last the clock indicated ten minutes past the hour. Young Scuddamore's spirit began to rise; he peered round the corner and saw no one at the place of meeting; doubtless his unknown correspondent had wearied and gone away. He became as bold as he had been formerly timid. It seemed to him that if he came at all to the appointment, however late, he was clear from the charge of cowardice. Nay, now he began to suspect a hoax, and actually complimented himself on his shrewdness in having suspected and out-manoeuvred his mystifiers. So very idle a thing is a boy's mind!

Armed with these reflections, he advanced boldly from his corner; but he had not taken above a couple of steps before a hand was laid upon his arm. He turned and beheld a lady cast in a very large mould and with somewhat stately features, but bearing no mark of severity in her looks.

"I see that you are a very self-confident lady-killer," said she; "for you make yourself expected. But I was determined to meet you. When a woman has once so far forgotten herself as to make the first advance, she has long ago left behind her all considerations of petty pride."

Silas was overwhelmed by the size and attractions of his correspondent and the suddenness with which she had fallen upon him. But she soon set him at his ease. She was very towardly and lenient in her behaviour; she led him on to make pleasantries, and then applauded him to the echo; and in a very short time, between blandishments and a liberal exhibition of warm brandy, she had not only induced him to fancy himself in love, but to declare his passion with the greatest vehemence.

"Alas!" she said; "I do not know whether I ought not to deplore this moment, great as is the pleasure you give me by your words. Hitherto I was alone to suffer; now, poor boy, there will be two. I am not my own mistress. I dare not ask you to visit me at my own house, for I am watched by jealous eyes. Let me see," she added; "I am older than you, although so much weaker; and while I trust in your courage and determination, I must employ my own knowledge of the world for our mutual benefit. Where do you live?"

He told her that he lodged in a furnished hotel, and named the street and number.

She seemed to reflect for some minutes, with an effort of mind.

"I see," she said at last. "You will be faithful and obedient, will you not?"

Silas assured her eagerly of his fidelity.

"Tomorrow night, then," she continued, with an encouraging smile, "you must remain at home, all the evening; and if any friends should visit you, dismiss them at once on any pretext that most readily presents itself. Your door is probably shut by ten?" she asked.

"By eleven," answered Silas.

"At a quarter-past eleven," pursued the lady, "leave the house. Merely cry for the door to be opened, and be sure you fall into no talk with the porter, as that might ruin everything. Go straight to the corner where the Luxembourg Gardens join the Boulevard; there you will find me waiting you. I trust you to follow my advice from point to point: and remember, if you fail me in only one particular, you will bring the sharpest trouble on a woman whose only fault is to have seen and loved you."

"I cannot see the use of all these instructions," said Silas.

"I believe you are already beginning to treat me as a master," she cried, tapping him with her fan upon the arm. "Patience, patience! that should come in time. A woman loves to be obeyed at first, although afterwards she finds her pleasure in obeying. Do as I ask you, for Heaven's sake, or I will answer for nothing. Indeed, now I think of it," she added, with the manner of one who has just seen further into a difficulty, "I find a better plan of keeping importunate visitors away. Tell the porter to admit no one for you, except a person who may come that night to claim a debt; and speak with some feeling, as though you feared the interview, so that he may take your words in earnest."

"I think you may trust me to protect myself against intruders," he said, not without a little pique.

"That is how I should prefer the thing arranged," she answered coldly. "I know you men; you think nothing of a woman's reputation."

Silas blushed and somewhat hung his head; for the scheme he had in view had involved a little vain-glorying before his acquaintances.

"Above all," she added, "do not speak to the porter as you come out."

"And why?" said he. "Of all your instructions, that seems to me the least important."

"You at first doubted the wisdom of some of the others, which you now see to be very necessary," she replied. "Believe me, this of your affection if you refuse me such trifles at our first interview?"

Silas confounded himself in explanations and apologies; in the middle of these she looked up at the clock and clapped her hands together with a suppressed scream.

"Heavens!" she cried, "is it so late? I have not an instant to lose. Alas, we poor women, what slaves we are! What have I not risked for you already?"

And after repeating her directions, which she artfully combined with caresses and the most abandoned looks, she bade him farewell and disappeared among the crowd.

The whole of the next day Silas was filled with a

sense of great importance; he was now sure she was a countess; and when evening came he minutely obeyed her orders and was at the corner of the Luxembourg Gardens by the hour appointed. No one was there. He waited nearly half an hour, looking in the face of every one who passed or loitered near the spot; he even visited the neighbouring corners of the Boulevard and made a complete circuit of the garden railings; but there was no beautiful countess to throw herself into his arms. At last, and most reluctantly, he began to retrace his steps towards his hotel. On the way he remembered the words he had heard pass between Madame Zéphyrile and the blond young man, and they gave him an indefinite uneasiness.

"It appears," he reflected, "that everyone has to tell lies to our porter."

He rang the bell, the door opened before him, and the porter in his bed-clothes came to offer him a light.

"Has he gone?" inquired the porter.

"He? Whom do you mean?" asked Silas, somewhat sharply, for he was irritated by his disappointment.

"I did not notice him go out," continued the porter, "but I trust you paid him. We do not care, in this house, to have lodgers who cannot meet their liabilities."

"What the devil do you mean?" demanded Silas rudely. "I cannot understand a word of this farrago."

"The short blond young man who came for his debt," returned the other. "Him it is I mean. Who else should it be, when I heard your orders to admit no one else?"

"Why, good God, of course he never came," retorted Silas.

"I believe what I believe," returned the porter, putting his tongue into his cheek with a most roguish air.

"You are an insolent scoundrel," cried Silas, and, feeling that he had made a ridiculous exhibition of asperity, and at the same time bewildered by a dozen alarms, he turned and began to run upstairs.

"Do you not want a light, then?" cried the porter.

But Silas only hurried the faster, and did not pause until he had reached the seventh landing and stood in front of his own door. There he waited a moment to recover his breath, assailed by the worst forebodings and almost dreading to enter the room.

When at last he did so he was relieved to find it dark and, to all appearance, untenanted. He drew a long breath. Here he was, home again in safety, and this should be his last folly as certainly as it had been his first. The matches stood on a little table by the bed, and he began to grope his way in that direction. As he moved his apprehensions grew upon him once more, and he was pleased, when his foot encountered an obstacle, to find it nothing more alarming than a chair. At last he touched curtains. From the position of the window, which was faintly visible, he knew he must be at the foot of the bed, and had only to feel his way along it in order to reach the table in question.

He lowered his hand, but what it touched was not simply a counterpane—it was a counterpane with something underneath it like the outline of a human leg. Silas withdrew his arm and stood a moment petrified.

"What, what," he thought, "can this betoken?"

He listened intently, but there was no sound of breathing. Once more, with a great effort, he reached out the end of his finger to the spot he had already touched; but this time he leaped back half a yard, and stood shivering and fixed with terror. There was something in his bed. What it was he knew not, but there was something there.

It was some seconds before he could move. Then, guided by an instinct, he fell straight upon the matches, and keeping his back towards the bed lighted a candle. As soon as the flame had kindled, he turned slowly round and looked for what he feared to see. Sure enough, there was the worst of his imaginations realized. The coverlid was drawn carefully up over the pillow, but it moulded the outline of a human body lying motionless; and when he dashed forward and flung aside the sheets, he beheld the blond young man whom he had seen in the Bullier Ball the night before, his eyes open and without speculation, his face swollen and blackened, and a thin stream of blood trickling from his nostrils.

Silas uttered a long, tremulous wail, dropped the candle, and fell on his knees beside the bed.

Silas was awakened from the stupor into which his terrible discovery had plunged him by a prolonged but discreet tapping at the door. It took him some seconds to remember his position; and when he hastened to prevent anyone from entering it was already too late. Dr Noel, in a tall nightcap, carrying a lamp which lighted up his long white countenance, sidling in his gait, and peering and cocking his head like some sort of bird, pushed the door slowly open, and advanced into the middle of the room.

"I thought I heard a cry," began the Doctor, "and fearing you might be unwell I did not hesitate to order this intrusion."

Silas, with a flushed face and a fearful beating heart, kept between the Doctor and the bed; but he found no voice to answer.

"You are in the dark," pursued the Doctor; "and yet you have not even begun to prepare for rest. You will not easily persuade me against my own eyesight; and your face declares most eloquently that you require either a friend or a physician—which is it to be? Let me feel your pulse, for that is often a just reporter of the heart."

He advanced to Silas, who still retreated before him backwards, and sought to take him by the wrist; but the strain on the young American's nerves had become too great for endurance. He avoided the Doctor with a febrile movement, and, throwing himself upon the floor, burst into a flood of weeping.

As soon as Dr Noel perceived the dead man in the bed his face darkened; and hurrying back to the door, which he had left ajar, he hastily closed and double locked it.

"Up!" he cried, addressing Silas in strident tones; "this is no time for weeping. What have you done? How came this body in your room? Speak freely to one who may be helpful. Do you imagine I would ruin you? Do you think this piece of dead flesh on your pillow can alter in any degree the sympathy with which you have inspired me? Credulous youth, the horror with which blind and unjust law regards an action never attaches to the doer in the eyes of those who love him; and if I saw the friend of my heart return to me out of seas of blood he would be in no way changed in my affection. Raise yourself," he said; "good and ill are a chimera; there is naught in life except destiny, and however you may be circumstanced there is one at your side who will help you to the last."

Thus encouraged, Silas gathered himself together,

and in a broken voice, and helped out by the Doctor's interrogations, contrived at last to put him in possession of the facts. But the conversation between the Prince and Geraldine he altogether omitted, as he had understood little of its purport, and had no idea that it was in any way related to his own misadventure.

"Alas!" cried Dr Noel, "I am much abused, or you have fallen innocently into the most dangerous hands in Europe. Poor boy, what a pit has been dug for your simplicity! into what a deadly peril have your unwary feet been conducted! This man," he said, "this Englishman, whom you twice saw, and whom I suspect to be the soul of the contrivance, can you describe him? Was he young or old? tall or short?"

But Silas, who, for all his curiosity, had not a seeing eye in his head, was able to supply nothing but meagre generalities, which it was impossible to recognize.

"I would have it a piece of education in all schools!" cried the Doctor angrily. "Where is the use of eyesight and articulate speech if a man cannot observe and recollect the features of his enemy? I, who know all the gangs of Europe, might have identified him, and gained new weapons for your defence. Cultivate this art in future, my poor boy; you may find it of momentous service."

"The future!" repeated Silas. "What future is there left for me except the gallows?"

"Youth is but a cowardly season," returned the Doctor; "and a man's own troubles look blacker than they are. I am old, and yet I never despair."

"Can I tell such a story to the police?" demanded Silas.

"Assuredly not," replied the Doctor. "From what I

see already of the machination in which you have been involved, your case is desperate upon that side; and for the narrow eye of the authorities you are infallibly the guilty person. And remember that we only know a portion of the plot; and the same infamous contrivers have doubtless arranged many other circumstances which would be elicited by a police inquiry, and help to fix the guilt more certainly upon your innocence.

"I am then lost, indeed!" cried Silas.

"I have not said so," answered Dr Noel, "for I am a cautious man."

"But look at this!" objected Silas, pointing to the body. "Here is this object in my bed; not to be explained, not to be disposed of, not to be regarded without horror."

"Horror?" replied the Doctor. "No. When this sort of clock has run down, it is no more to me than an ingenious piece of mechanism, to be investigated with the bistoury. When blood is once cold and stagnant, it is no longer human blood; when flesh is once dead, it is no longer that flesh which we desire in our lovers and respect in our friends. The grace, the attraction, the terror, have all gone from it with the animating spirit. Accustom yourself to look upon it with composure; for if my scheme is practicable you will have to live some days in constant proximity to that which now so greatly horrifies you."

"Your scheme?" cried Silas. "What is that? Tell me speedily, Doctor; for I have scarcely courage enough to continue to exist." Without replying, Dr Noel turned towards the bed, and proceeded to examine the corpse.

"Quite dead," he murmured. "Yes, as I had supposed, the pockets empty. Yes, and the name cut off the shirt. Their work has been done thoroughly and well. Fortunately, he is of small stature."

Silas followed these words with an extreme anxiety. At last the Doctor, his autopsy completed, took a chair and addressed the young American with a smile.

"Since I came into your room" said he, "although my ears and my tongue have been so busy, I have not suffered my eyes to remain idle. I noticed a little while ago that you have there, in the corner, one of those monstrous constructions which your fellow countrymen carry with them into all quarters of the globe—in a word, a Saratoga trunk. Until this moment I have never been able to conceive the utility of these erections; but then I began to have a glimmer. Whether it was for convenience in the slave trade, or to obviate the results of too ready an employment of the bowie knife, I cannot bring myself to decide. But one thing I see plainly—the object of such a box is to contain a human body."

"Surely," cried Silas, "surely this is not a time for jesting."

"Although I may express myself with some degree of pleasantry," replied the Doctor, "the purport of my words is entirely serious. And the first thing we have to do, my young friend, is to empty your coffer of all that it contains."

Silas, obeying the authority of Dr Noel, put himself at his disposition. The Saratoga trunk was soon gutted of its contents, which made a considerable litter on the floor; and then—Silas taking the heels and the Doctor supporting the shoulders—the body of the murdered man was carried from the bed, and, after some difficulty, doubled up and inserted whole into the empty box. With an effort on the part of both, the lid was forced down upon this unusual baggage, and the trunk was locked and corded by the Doctor's own hand, while Silas disposed of what had been taken out between the closet and a chest of drawers.

"Now," said the Doctor, "the first step has been taken on the way to your deliverance. Tomorrow, or rather today, it must be your task to allay the suspicions of your porter, paying him all that you owe; while you may trust me to make the arrangements necessary to a safe conclusion. Meantime, follow me to my room, where I shall give you a safe and powerful opiate; for whatever you do, you must have rest."

The next day was the longest in Silas's memory; it seemed as if it would never be done. He denied himself to his friends, and sat in a corner with his eyes fixed upon the Saratoga trunk, in dismal contemplation. His own former indiscretions were now returned upon him in kind; for the observatory had been once more opened, and he was conscious of an almost continual study from Madame Zéphyrile's apartment. So distressing did this become, that he was at last obliged to block up the spy-hole from his own side; and when he was thus secured from observation he spent a considerable portion of his time in contrite tears and prayer.

Late in the evening Dr Noel entered the room carrying in his hand a pair of sealed envelopes without address, one somewhat bulky, and the other so slim as to seem without enclosure.

"Silas," he said, seating himself at the table, "the time has now come for me to explain my plan for your salvation. Tomorrow morning at an early hour, Prince

Florizel of Bohemia returns to London, after having diverted himself for a few days with the Parisian Carnival. It was my fortune, a good while ago, to do Colonel Geraldine, his Master of the Horse, one of those services, so common in my profession, which are never forgotten upon either side. I have no need to explain to you the nature of the obligation under which he was laid; suffice it to say that I knew him ready to serve me in any practicable manner. Now, it was necessary for you to gain London with your trunk unopened. To this the Custom House seemed to oppose a fatal difficulty; but I bethought me that the baggage of so considerable a person as the Prince is, as a matter of courtesy, passed without examination by the officers of Custom. I applied to Colonel Geraldine, and succeeded in obtaining a favourable answer. Tomorrow, if you go before six to the hotel where the Prince lodges, your baggage will be passed over as a part of his, and you yourself will make the journey as a member of his suite.

"It seems to me, as you speak, that I have already seen both the Prince and Colonel Geraldine; I even overheard some of their conversation the other evening at the Bullier Ball."

"It is probably enough; for the Prince loves to mix with all societies," replied the Doctor. "Once arrived in London," he pursued, "your task is nearly ended. In this more bulky envelope I have given you a letter which I dare not address; but in the other you will find the designation of the house to which you must carry it along with your box, which will there be taken from you and not trouble you any more."

"Alas!" said Silas, "I have every wish to believe you; but how is it possible? You open up to me a bright prospect, but, I ask you, is my mind capable of receiving so unlikely a solution. Be more generous, and let me further understand your meaning."

The Doctor seemed painfully impressed.

"Boy," he answered, "you do not know how hard a thing you ask of me. But be it so. I am now inured to humiliation; and it would be strange if I refused you this, after having granted you so much. Know then, that although I now make so quiet an appearance— frugal, solitary, addicted to study—when I was younger my name was once a rallying-cry among the most astute and dangerous spirits of London; and while I was outwardly an object of respect and consideration, my true power resided in the most secret, terrible, and criminal relations. It is to one of the persons who then obeyed me that I now address myself to deliver you from your burden. They were men of many different nations and dexterities, all bound together by a formidable oath, and working for the same purpose; the trade of the association was in murder; and I who speak to you, innocent as I appear, was the chieftain of this redoubtable crew."

"What?" cried Silas. "A murderer? And one with whom murder was a trade? Can I take your hand? Ought I so much as to accept your services? Dark and criminal old man, would you make an accomplice of my youth and my distress?"

The Doctor bitterly laughed.

"You are difficult to please, Mr Scuddamore," said he; "but I now offer you your choice of company between the murdered man and the murderer. If your conscience is too nice to accept my aid, say so, and I will immediately leave you. Thenceforward you can deal with your trunk and its belongings as best suits your upright conscience."

"I own myself wrong" replied Silas. I should have remembered how generously you offered to shield me, even before I had convinced you of my innocence, and I continue to listen to your counsels with gratitude."

"That is well," returned the Doctor; "and I perceive you are beginning to learn some of the lessons of experience."

"At the same time," resumed the New Englander, "as you confess yourself accustomed to this tragical business, and the people to whom you recommend me are your own former associates and friends, could you not yourself undertake the transport of the box, and rid me at once of its detested presence?"

"Upon my word," replied the Doctor, "I admire you cordially. If you do not think I have already meddled sufficiently in your concerns, believe me, from my heart I think the contrary. Take or leave my services as I offer them; and trouble me with no more words of gratitude, for I value your consideration even more lightly than I do your intellect. A time will come, if you should be spared to see a number of years in health of mind, when you will think differently of all this, and blush for your tonight's behaviour."

So saying, the Doctor arose from his chair, repeated his directions briefly and clearly, and departed from the room without permitting Silas any time to answer.

The next morning Silas presented himself at the hotel, where he was politely received by Colonel Geraldine, and relieved, from that moment, of all immediate alarm about his trunk and its grisly contents. The journey passed over without much incident, although the young man was horrified to overhear the

sailors and railway porters complaining among themselves about the unusual weight of the Prince's baggage. Silas travelled in a carriage with the valets, for
Prince Florizel chose to be alone with his Master of the
Horse.

On board the steamer, however, Silas attracted his
Highness's attention by the melancholy of his air and
attitude as he stood gazing at the pile of baggage; for
he was still full of disquietude about the future.

"There is a young man," observed the Prince, "who
must have some cause for sorrow."

"That," replied Geraldine, "is the American for
whom I obtained permission to travel with your suite."

"You remind me that I have been remiss in courtesy," said Prince Florizel, and advancing to Silas, he
addressed him with the most exquisite condescension
in these words:

"I was charmed, young sir, to be able to gratify the
desire you made known to me through Colonel
Geraldine. Remember, if you please, that I shall be
glad at any future time to lay you under a more serious
obligation."

And then he put some questions as to the political
condition of America, which Silas answered with
sense and propriety.

"You are still a young man," said the Prince; "but I
observe you to be very serious for your years. Perhaps
you allow your attention to be too much occupied with
grave studies. But perhaps, on the other hand, I am
myself indiscreet and touch upon a painful subject."

"I have certainly cause to be the most miserable of
men, said Silas; "never has a more innocent person
been more dismally abused."

"I will not ask you for your confidence," returned Prince Florizel. "But do not forget that Colonel Geraldine's recommendation is an unfailing passport; and that I am not only willing, but possibly more able than many others, to do you a service."

Silas was delighted with the amiability of this great personage; but his mind soon returned upon its gloomy preoccupations; for not even the favour of a Prince to a Republican can discharge a brooding spirit of its cares.

The train arrived at Charing Cross, where the officers of the Revenue respected the baggage of Prince Florizel in the usual manner. The most elegant equipages were in waiting; and Silas was driven, along with the rest, to the Prince's residence. There Colonel Geraldine sought him out, and expressed himself pleased to have been of any service to a friend of the physician's, for whom he professed a great consideration.

"I hope," he added, "that you will find none of your porcelain injured. Special orders were given along the line to deal tenderly with the Prince's effects."

And then, directing the servants to place one of the carriages at the young gentleman's disposal, and at once to charge the Saratoga trunk upon the dickey, the Colonel shook hands and excused himself on account of his occupations in the princely household.

Silas now broke the seal of the envelope containing the address, and directed the stately footman to drive him to Box Court, opening off the Strand. It seemed as if the place were not at all unknown to the man, for he looked startled and begged a repetition of the order. It was with a heart full of alarms that Silas mounted into the luxurious vehicle, and was driven to his destination. The entrance to Box Court was too narrow for the passage of a coach; it was a mere footway between railings, with a post at either end.

On one of these posts was seated a man, who at once jumped down and exchanged a friendly sign with the driver, while the footman opened the door and inquired of Silas whether he should take down the Saratoga trunk, and to what number it should be carried.

"If you please," said Silas. "To number three."

The footman and the man who had been sitting on the post, even with the aid of Silas himself, had hard work to carry the trunk; and before it was deposited at the door of the house in question, the young American was horrified to find a score of loiterers looking on. But he knocked with as good a countenance as he could muster up, and presented the other envelope to him who opened.

"He is not at home," said he, "but if you will leave your letter and return tomorrow early, I shall be able to inform you whether and when he can receive your visit. Would you like to leave your box?" he added.

"Dearly," cried Silas; and the next moment he repented his precipitation, and declared, with equal emphasis, that he would rather carry the box along with him to the hotel.

The crowd jeered at his indecision and followed him to the carriage with insulting remarks; and Silas, covered with shame and terror, implored the servants to conduct him to some quiet and comfortable house of entertainment in the immediate neighbourhood.

The Prince's equipage deposited Silas at the Craven Hotel in Craven Street, and immediately drove away, leaving him alone with the servants of the inn. The only vacant room, it appeared, was a little den up four pairs of stairs, and looking towards the back. To this hermitage, with infinite trouble and complaint, a pair of stout porters carried the Saratoga trunk. It is needless to mention that Silas kept closely at their heels throughout the ascent, and had his heart in his mouth at every corner. A single false step, he reflected. and the box might go over the banisters and land its fatal contents, plainly discovered, on the pavement of the hall.

Arrived in the room, he sat down on the edge of his bed to recover from the agony that he had just endured; but he had hardly taken his position when he was recalled to a sense of his peril by the action of the boots, who had knelt beside the trunk, and was proceeding officiously to undo its elaborate fastenings.

"Let it be!" cried Silas. "I shall want nothing from it while I stay here."

"You might have let it lie in the hall, then," growled the man; "a thing as big and heavy as a church. What you have inside I cannot fancy. If it is all money, you are a richer man than me."

"Money?" repeated Silas, in a sudden perturbation. "What do you mean by money? I have no money, and you are speaking like a fool."

"All right, captain," retorted the boots with a wink. "There's nobody will touch your lordship's money. I'm as safe as the bank," he added; "but as the box is heavy, I shouldn't mind drinking something to your lordship's health."

Silas pressed two Napoleons upon his acceptance, apologizing, at the same time, for being obliged to trouble him with foreign money, and pleading his recent arrival for excuse. And the man, grumbling with even greater fervour, and looking contemptuously from the money in his hand to the Saratoga trunk and back again from the one to the other, at last consented to withdraw.

For nearly two days the dead body had been packed into Silas's box; and as soon as he was alone the unfortunate New Englander nosed all the cracks and openings with the most passionate attention. But the weather was cool, and the trunk still managed to contain his shocking secret.

He took a chair beside it, and buried his face in his hands, and his mind in the most profound reflection. If he were not speedily relieved, no question but he must be speedily discovered. Alone, in a strange city, without friends or accomplices, if the Doctor's introduction failed him, he was indubitably a lost New Englander. He reflected pathetically over his ambitious designs for the future; he should not now become the hero and spokesman of his native place of Bangor, Maine; he should not, as he had fondly anticipated, move on from office to office, from honour to honour; he might as well divest himself at once of all hope of being acclaimed President of the United States, and leaving behind him a statue, in the worst possible style of art, to adorn the Capitol at Washington. Here he was, chained to a dead Englishman doubled up inside a Saratoga trunk; whom he must get rid of, or perish from the rolls of national glory!

I should be afraid to chronicle the language employed by this young man to the Doctor, to the murdered man, to Madame Zéphyrine, to the boots of the hotel, to the Prince's servants, and, in a word, to all who had been ever so remotely connected with his horrible misfortune.

He slunk down to dinner about seven at night; but the yellow coffee-room appalled him, the eyes of the other diners seemed to rest on his with suspicion, and his mind remained upstairs with the Saratoga trunk. When the waiter came to offer him cheese, his nerves were already so much on edge that he leaped half-way out of his chair and upset the remainder of a pint of ale upon the table-cloth.

The fellow offered to show him to the smoking-room when he had done, and although he would have much preferred to return at once to his perilous treasure, he had not the courage to refuse, and was shown downstairs to the black, gas-lit cellar, which formed, and possibly still forms, the divan of the Craven Hotel.

Two very sad betting men were playing billiards, attended by a moist, consumptive marker; and for the moment Silas imagined that these were the only occupants of the apartment. But at the next glance his eye fell upon a person smoking in the farthest corner, with lowered eyes and a most respectable and modest aspect. He knew at once that he had seen the face before; and, in spite of the entire change of clothes, recognized the man whom he had found seated on a post at the entrance to Box Court, and who had helped him to carry the trunk to and from the carriage. The New Englander simply turned and ran, nor did he pause until he had locked and bolted himself into his bedroom.

There, all night long, a prey to the most terrible imaginations, he watched beside the fatal boxful of dead flesh. The suggestion of the boots that his trunk was full of gold inspired him with all manner of new terrors, if he so much as dared to close an eye; and the presence in the smoking-room, and under an obvious disguise, of the loiterer from Box Court convinced him that he was once more the centre of obscure machinations.

Midnight had sounded some time, when, impelled by uneasy suspicions, Silas opened his bedroom door and peered into the passage. It was dimly illuminated by a single jet of gas; and some distance off he perceived a man sleeping on the floor in the costume of an hotel under-servant. Silas drew near the man on tiptoe. He lay partly on his back, partly on his side, and his right forearm concealed his face from recognition. Suddenly, while the American was still bending over him, the sleeper removed his arm and opened his eyes, and Silas found himself once more face to face with the loiterer of Box Court.

"Good night, sir," said the man pleasantly.

But Silas was too profoundly moved to find an answer, and regained his room in silence.

Towards morning, worn out by apprehension, he fell asleep on his chair, with his head forward on the trunk. In spite of so constrained an attitude and such a grisly pillow, his slumber was sound and prolonged, and he was only awakened at a late hour by a sharp tapping at the door.

He hurried to open, and found the boots without.

"You are the gentleman who called yesterday at Box Court?" he asked.

Silas, with a quiver, admitted that he had done so.

"Then this note is for you," added the servant, proffering a sealed envelope.

Silas tore it open, and found inside the words: "Twelve o'clock."

He was punctual to the hour; the trunk was carried before him by several stout servants; and he was himself ushered into a room, where a man sat warming himself before the fire with his back towards the door. The sound of so many persons entering and leaving, and the scraping of the trunk as it was deposited upon the bare boards, were alike unable to attract the notice of the occupant; and Silas stood waiting, in an agony of fear, until he should deign to recognize his presence.

Perhaps five minutes had elapsed before the man turned leisurely about, and disclosed the features of Prince Florizel of Bohemia.

"So, sir," he said, with great severity, "this is the manner in which you abuse my politeness. You join yourself to persons of condition, I perceive, for no other purpose than to escape the consequences of your crimes; and I can readily understand your embarrassment when I addressed myself to you yesterday."

"Indeed," cried Silas, "I am innocent of everything except misfortune."

And in a hurried voice, and with the greatest ingenuousness, he recounted to the Prince the whole history of his calamity.

"I see I have been mistaken," said his Highness, when he had heard him to an end. "You are no other than a victim, and since I am not to punish you you may be sure I shall do my utmost to help. And now," he continued, "to business. Open your box at once, and let me see what it contains."

Silas changed colour.

"I almost fear to look upon it," he exclaimed.

"Nay," replied the Prince, "have you not looked at it already? This is a form of sentimentality to be resisted. The sight of a sick man, whom we can still help, should appeal more directly to the feelings than that of a dead man who is equally beyond help or harm, love or hatred. Nerve yourself, Mr Scuddamore," and then, seeing that Silas still hesitated, "I do not desire to give another name to my request," he added.

The young American awoke as if out of a dream, and with a shiver of repugnance addressed himself to loose the straps and open the lock of the Saratoga trunk. The Prince stood by, watching with a composed countenance and his hands behind his back. The body was quite stiff, and it cost Silas a great effort, both moral and physical to dislodge it from its position and discover the face.

Prince Florizel started back with an exclamation of painful surprise.

"Alas," he cried, "you little know, Mr Scuddamore, what a cruel gift you have brought me. This is a young man of my own suite, the brother of my trusted friend; and it was upon matters of my own service that he had thus perished at the hands of violent and treacherous men. Poor Geraldine," he went on, as if to himself, "in what words am I to tell you of your brother's fate? How can I excuse myself in your eyes, or in the eyes of God, for the presumptuous schemes that led him to this bloody and unnatural death? Ah, Florizel! Florizel! when will you learn the discretion that suits mortal life, and be no longer dazzled with the image of power at your disposal? Power!" he cried; "who is more powerless? I look upon this young man whom I have sacrificed, Mr Scuddamore, and feel how small a thing it is to be a Prince."

Silas was moved at the sight of his emotion. He tried to murmur some consolatory words, and burst into tears. The Prince, touched by his obvious intention, came up to him and took him by the hand.

"Command yourself," said he. "We have both much to learn, and we shall both be better men for today's meeting."

Silas thanked him in silence with an affectionate look.

"Write me the address of Dr Noel on this piece of paper," continued the Prince, leading him towards the table; "and let me recommend you, when you are again in Paris, to avoid the society of that dangerous man. He has acted in this matter on a generous inspiration— that I must believe; had he been privy to young Geraldine's death he would never have dispatched the body to the care of the actual criminal."

"The actual criminal!" repeated Silas in astonishment.

"Even so," returned the Prince. "This letter, which the disposition of Almighty Providence has so strangely delivered into my hands, was addressed to no less a person than the criminal himself, the infamous President of the Suicide Club. Seek to pry no further in these perilous affairs, but content yourself with your own miraculous escape, and leave this house at once. I have pressing affairs, and must arrange at once about this poor clay, which was so lately a gallant and handsome youth."

Silas took a grateful and submissive leave of Prince Florizel, but he lingered in Box Court until he saw him depart in a splendid carriage on a visit to Colonel Henderson of the police. Republican as he was, the young American took off his hat with almost a sentimental devotion to the retreating carriage. And the same night he started by rail on his return to Paris.

Here (observes my Arabian author) *is the end of the* HISTORY OF THE PHYSICIAN AND THE SARATOGA TRUNK. *Omitting some reflections on the power of Providence, highly pertinent in the original, but little suited to our occidental taste, I shall only add that Mr Scuddamore has already begun to mount the ladder of political fame, and by last advices was the Sheriff of his native town.*

3

The Adventure of the Hansom Cabs

Lieutenant Brackenbury Rich had greatly distinguished himself in one of the lesser Indian hill wars. He it was who took the chieftain prisoner with his own hand; his gallantry was universally applauded; and when he came home, prostrated by an ugly sabre cut and a protracted jungle fever, society was prepared to welcome the Lieutenant as a celebrity of minor lustre. But his was a character remarkable for unaffected modesty; adventure was dear to his heart, but he cared little for adulation; and he waited at foreign watering-places and in Algiers until the fame of his exploits had run through its nine days' vitality and begun to be forgotten. He arrived in London at last, in the early season, with as little observation as he could desire; and as he was an orphan and had none but distant relatives who lived in the provinces, it was almost as a foreigner that he installed himself in the capital of the country for which he had shed his blood.

On the day following his arrival he dined alone at a military club. He shook hands with a few old comrades, and received their warm congratulations; but as one and all had some engagement for the evening, he found himself left entirely to his own resources. He was in dress, for he had entertained the notion of visiting a theatre. But the great city was new to him; he had gone from a provincial school to a military college, and thence direct to the Eastern Empire; and he promised himself a variety of delights in this world for exploration. Swinging his cane, he took his way westward. It was a mild evening, already dark, and now and then threatening rain. The succession of faces in the lamplight stirred the Lieutenant's imagination; and it seemed to him as if he could walk for ever in that stimulating city atmosphere and surrounded by the mystery of our million private lives. He glanced at the houses, and marvelled what was passing behind those warmly lighted windows; he looked into face after face, and saw them each intent upon some unknown interest, criminal or kindly.

"They talk of war," he thought, "but this is the great battlefield of mankind."

And then he began to wonder that he should walk so long in this complicated scene, and not chance upon so much as the shadow of an adventure for himself

"All in good time," he reflected. "I am still a stranger, and perhaps wear a strange air. But I must be drawn into the eddy before long."

The night was already well advanced when a plump of cold rain fell suddenly out of the darkness. Brackenbury paused under some trees, and as he did so he caught sight of a hansom cabman making him a sign that he was disengaged. The circumstance fell in so happily to the occasion that he at once raised his cane in answer, and had soon ensconced himself in the London gondola.

"Where to, sir?" asked the driver.

"Where you please," said Brackenbury.

And immediately, at a pace of surprising swiftness,

the hansom drove off through the rain into a maze of villas. One villa was so like another, each with its front garden, and there was so little to distinguish the deserted lamp-lit streets and crescents through which the flying hansom took its way, that Brackenbury soon lost all idea of direction. He would have been tempted to believe that the cabman was amusing himself by driving him round and round and in and out about a small quarter, but there was something businesslike in the speed which convinced him of the contrary. The man had an object in view, he was hastening towards a definite end; and Brackenbury was at once astonished at the fellow's skill in picking a way through such a labyrinth, and a little concerned to imagine what was the occasion of his hurry. He had heard tales of strangers falling ill in London. Did the driver belong to some bloody and treacherous association? and was he himself being whirled to a murderous death?

The thought had scarcely presented itself, when the cab swung sharply round a corner and pulled up before the garden gate of a villa in a long and wide road. The house was brilliantly lighted up. Another hansom had just driven away, and Brackenbury could see a gentleman being admitted at the front door and received by several liveried servants. He was surprised that the cabman should have stopped so immediately in front of a house where a reception was being held; but he did not doubt it was the result of accident, and sat placidly smoking where he was until he heard the trap thrown open over his head.

"Here we are, sir," said the driver.

"Here!" repeated Brackenbury. "Where?"

"You told me to take you where I pleased, sir," returned the man with a chuckle, "and here we are."

It struck Brackenbury that the voice was wonderfully smooth and courteous for a man in so inferior a position; he remembered the speed at which he had been driven; and now it occurred to him that the hansom was more luxuriously appointed than the common run of public conveyances.

"I must ask you to explain," said he. "Do you mean to turn me out into the rain? My good man, I suspect the choice is mine."

"The choice is certainly yours," replied the driver; "but when I tell you all, I believe I know how a gentleman of your figure will decide. There is a gentleman's party in this house. I do not know whether the master be a stranger to London and without acquaintances of his own; or whether he is a man of odd notions. But certainly I was hired to kidnap single gentlemen in evening dress, as many as I pleased, but military officers by preference. You have simply to go in and say that Mr Morris invited you."

"Are you Mr Morris?" inquired the Lieutenant.

"Oh, no," replied the cabman. "Mr Morris is the person of the house."

"It is not a common way of collecting guests," said Brackenbury; "but an eccentric man might very well indulge the whim without any intention to offend. And suppose that I refuse Mr Morris's invitation," he went on, "what then?"

"My orders are to drive you back where I took you from," replied the man, "and set out to look for others up to midnight. Those who have no fancy for such an adventure, Mr Morris said, were not the guests for him."

These words decided the Lieutenant on the spot.

"After all," he reflected, as he descended from the hansom, "I have not had long to wait for my adventure."

He had hardly found footing on the side-walk, and was still feeling in his pocket for the fare, when the cab swung about and drove off by the way it came at the former break-neck velocity. Brackenbury shouted after the man, who paid no heed, and continued to drive away; but the sound of his voice was overheard in the house, the door was again thrown open, emitting a flood of light upon the garden, and a servant ran down to meet him holding an umbrella.

"The cabman has been paid," observed the servant in a very civil tone; and he proceeded to escort Brackenbury along the path and up the steps. In the hall several other attendants relieved him of his hat, cane, and paletot, gave him a ticket with a number in return, and politely hurried him up a stair adorned with tropical flowers, to the door of an apartment on the first story. Here a grave butler inquired his name, and announcing "Lieutenant Brackenbury Rich," ushered him into the drawing-room of the house.

A young man, slender and singularly handsome, came forward and greeted him with an air at once courtly and affectionate. Hundreds of candles of the finest wax, lit up a room that was perfumed, like the staircase, with a profusion of rare and beautiful flowering shrubs. A side-table was loaded with tempting viands. Several servants went to and fro with fruits and goblets of champagne. The company was perhaps sixteen in number, all men, few beyond the prime of life, and, with hardly an exception, of a dashing and capable exterior. They were divided into two groups, one about a roulette board, and the other surrounding a table at which one of their number held a bank at baccarat.

"I see," thought Brackenbury, "I am in a private gambling saloon, and the cabman was a tout."

His eye had embraced the details, and his mind formed the conclusion, while his host was still holding him by the hand; and to him his looks returned from this rapid survey. At a second view Mr Morris surprised him still more than on the first. The easy elegance of his manners, the distinction, amiability, and courage that appeared upon his features, fitted very ill with the Lieutenant's preconceptions on the subject of the proprietor of a hell; and the tone of his conversation seemed to mark him out for a man of position and merit. Brackenbury found he had an instinctive liking for his entertainer; and though he chided himself for the weakness, he was unable to resist a sort of friendly attraction for Mr Morris's person and character.

"I have heard of you, Lieutenant Rich," said Mr Morris, lowering his tone; "and believe me I am gratified to make your acquaintance. Your looks accord with the reputation that has preceded you from India. And if you will forget for a while the irregularity of your presentation in my house, I shall feel it not only an honour, but a genuine pleasure besides. A man who makes a mouthful of barbarian cavaliers," he added with a laugh, "should not be appalled by a breach of etiquette, however serious."

And he led him towards the sideboard and pressed him to partake of some refreshment.

"Upon my word," the Lieutenant reflected, "this is one of the pleasantest fellows and, I do not doubt, one of the most agreeable societies in London."

He partook of some champagne, which he found excellent; and observing that many of the company were already smoking, he lit one of his own Manilas, and strolled up to the roulette board, where he sometimes made a stake and sometimes looked on smilingly on the fortune of others. It was while he was thus idling that he became aware of a sharp scrutiny to which the whole of the guests were subjected. Mr Morris went here and there, ostensibly busied on hospitable concerns; but he had ever a shrewd glance at disposal; not a man of the party escaped his sudden, searching looks; he took stock of the bearing of heavy losers, he valued the amount of the stakes, he paused behind couples who were deep in conversation; and, in a word, there was hardly a characteristic of anyone present but he seemed to catch and make a note of it. Brackenbury began to wonder if this were indeed a gambling hell: it had so much the air of a private inquisition. He followed Mr Morris in all his movements; and although the man had a ready smile, he seemed to perceive, as it were under a mask, a haggard, careworn and preoccupied spirit. The fellows around him laughed and made their game; but Brackenbury had lost interest in the guests.

"This Morris," thought he, "is no idler in the room. Some deep purpose inspires him; let it be mine to fathom it."

Now and then Mr Morris would call one of his visitors aside; and after a brief colloquy in an ante-room, he would return alone, and the visitors in question reappeared no more. After a certain number of repetitions, this performance excited Brackenbury's curiosity to a high degree. He determined to be at the bottom of this minor mystery at once; and, strolling into the ante-room, found a deep window recess concealed by curtains of the fashionable green. Here he hurriedly ensconced himself; nor had he to wait long before the sound of steps and voices drew near him from the principal apartment. Peering through the division, he saw Mr Morris escorting a fat and ruddy personage, with somewhat the look of a commercial traveller, whom Brackenbury had already remarked for his coarse laugh and under-bred behaviour at the table. The pair halted immediately before the window, so that Brackenbury lost not a word of the following discourse:

"I beg you a thousand pardons!" began Mr Morris, with the most conciliatory manner; "and, if I appear rude, I am sure you will readily forgive me. In a place so great as London accidents must continually happen; and the best that we can hope is to remedy them with as small delay as possible. I will not deny that I fear you have made a mistake and honoured my poor house by inadvertence; for, to speak openly, I cannot at all remember your appearance. Let me put the question without unnecessary circumlocution—between gentlemen of honour a word will suffice—Under whose roof do you suppose yourself to be?"

"That of Mr Morris," replied the other, with a prodigious display of confusion, which had been visibly growing upon him throughout the last few words.

"Mr John or Mr James Morris?" inquired the host.

"I really cannot tell you," returned the unfortunate guest. "I am not personally acquainted with the gentleman, any more than I am with yourself"

"I see," said Mr Morris. "There is another person of the same name farther down the street; and I have no doubt the policeman will be able to supply you with his number. Believe me, I felicitate myself on the misunderstanding which has procured me the pleasure of your company for so long; and let me express a hope that we may meet again upon a more regular footing. Meantime, I would not for the world detain you longer from your friends. John," he added, raising his voice, "will you see that this gentleman finds his greatcoat?"

And with the most agreeable air Mr Morris escorted his visitor as far as the ante-room door, where he left him under conduct of the butler. As he passed the window, on his return to the drawing-room, Brackenbury could hear him utter a profound sigh, as though his mind was loaded with a great anxiety, and his nerves already fatigued with the task on which he was engaged.

For perhaps an hour the hansoms kept arriving with such frequency that Mr Morris had to receive a new guest for every old one that he sent away, and the company preserved its number undiminished. But towards the end of that time the arrivals grew few and far between, and at length ceased entirely, while the process of elimination was continued with unimpaired activity. The drawing-room began to look empty; the baccarat was discontinued for lack of a banker: more than one person said good night of his own accord, and was suffered to depart without expostulation; and in the meanwhile Mr Morris redoubled in agreeable attentions to those who stayed behind. He went from group to group and from person to person with looks of the readiest sympathy and the most pertinent and pleasing talk; he was not so much like a host as like a hostess and there was a feminine coquetry and condescension in his manner which charmed the hearts of all.

As the guests grew thinner, Lieutenant Rich strolled

for a moment out of the drawing-room into the hall in quest of fresher air. But he had no sooner passed the threshold of the ante-chamber than he was brought to a dead halt by a discovery of the most surprising nature. The flowering shrubs had disappeared from the staircase; three large furniture wagons stood before the garden gate; the servants were busy dismantling the house upon all sides; and some of them had already donned their greatcoats and were preparing to depart. It was like the end of a country ball, where everything has been supplied by contract. Brackenbury had indeed some matter for reflection. First, the guests, who were no real guests after all, had been dismissed; and now the servants, who could hardly be genuine servants, were actively dispersing.

"Was the whole establishment a sham?" he asked himself "The mushroom of a single night which should disappear before morning?"

Watching a favourable opportunity, Brackenbury dashed upstairs to the highest regions of the house. It was as he had expected. He ran from room to room, and saw not a stick of furniture nor so much as a picture on the walls. Although the house had been painted and papered, it was not only uninhabited at present, but plainly had never been inhabited at all. The young officer remembered with astonishment its specious, settled, and hospitable air on his arrival. It was only at a prodigious cost that the imposture could have been carried out upon so great a scale.

Who, then, was Mr Morris? What was his intention in thus playing the householder for a single night in the remote west of London? And why did he collect his visitors at hazard from the streets?

Brackenbury remembered that he had already de-
layed too long, and hastened to join the company.
Many had left during his absence; and counting the
Lieutenant and his host, there were not more than five
persons in the drawing-room—recently so thronged.
Mr Morris greeted him, as he re-entered the apartment,
with a smile, and immediately rose to his feet.

"It is now time, gentlemen," said he, "to explain my
purpose in decoying you from your amusements. I
trust you did not find the evening hang very dully on
your hands; but my object, I will confess it, was not
to entertain your leisure, but to help myself in an
unfortunate necessity. You are all gentlemen," he
continued, "your appearance does you that much
justice, and I ask for no better security. Hence, I
speak it without concealment, I ask you to render
me a dangerous and delicate service; dangerous because you may run the hazard of your lives, and delicate because I must ask an absolute discretion upon all
that you shall see or hear. From an utter stranger the request is almost comically extravagant; I am well aware
of this; and I would add at once, if there be anyone
present who has heard enough, if there be one among
the party who recoils from a dangerous confidence
and a piece of quixotic devotion to he knows not
whom—here is my hand ready, and I shall wish him
good night and God-speed with all the sincerity in
the world."

A very tall, black man, with a heavy stoop, immediately responded to this appeal.

"I commend your frankness, sir," said he; "and, for
my part, I go. I make no reflections; but I cannot deny
that you fill me with suspicious thoughts. I go myself,

as I say; and perhaps you will think I have no right to add words to my example."

"On the contrary," replied Mr Morris, "I am obliged to you for all you say. It would be impossible to exaggerate the gravity of my proposal."

"Well, gentlemen, what do you say?" said the tall man, addressing the others. "We have had our evening's frolic; shall we all go homeward peaceably in a body? You will think well of my suggestion in the morning, when you see the sun again in innocence and safety."

The speaker pronounced the last words with an intonation which added to their force; and his face wore a singular expression, full of gravity and significance. Another of the company rose hastily and, with some appearance of alarm, prepared to take his leave. There were only two who held their ground, Brackenbury and an old red-nosed cavalry Major; but these two preserved a nonchalant demeanour, and, beyond a look of intelligence which they rapidly exchanged, appeared entirely foreign to the discussion that had just been terminated.

Mr Morris conducted the deserters as far as the door, which he closed upon their heels; then he turned round, disclosing a countenance of mingled relief and animation, and addressed the two officers as follows:

"I have chosen my men like Joshua in the Bible," said Mr Morris "and now I believe I have the pick of London. Your appearance pleased my hansom cabmen; then it delighted me; I have watched your behaviour in a strange company, and under the most unusual circumstances: I have studied how you played and how you bore your losses; lastly, I have put you to the test of a staggering announcement, and you received it like an invitation to dinner. It is not for nothing," he cried, "that I have been for years the companion and the pupil of the bravest and wisest potentate in Europe."

"At the affair of Bunderchang," observed the Major, "I asked for twelve volunteers, and every trooper in the ranks replied to my appeal. But a gaming party is not the same thing as a regiment under fire. You may be pleased, I suppose, to have found two, and two who will not fail you at a push. As for the pair who ran away, I count them among the most pitiful hounds I ever met with. Lieutenant Rich," he added, addressing Brackenbury, "I have heard much of you of late; and I cannot doubt but you have also heard of me. I am Major O'Rooke."

And the veteran tendered his hand, which was red and tremulous, to the young Lieutenant.

"Who has not?" answered Brackenbury.

"When this little matter is settled," said Mr Morris, "you will think I have sufficiently rewarded you; for I could offer neither a more valuable service than to make him acquainted with the other."

"And now," said Major O'Rooke, "is it a duel?"

"A duel after a fashion," replied Mr Morris, "a duel with unknown and dangerous enemies, and, as I gravely fear, a duel to the death. I must ask you," he continued, "to call me Morris no longer; call me, if you please, Hammersmith; my real name, as well as that of another person to whom I hope to present you before long, you will gratify me by not asking and not seeking to discover for yourselves. Three days ago the person of whom I speak disappeared suddenly from home; and, until this morning, I received no hint of his situation. You will fancy my alarm when I tell you that he is engaged upon a work of private justice. Bound by an unhappy oath, too lightly sworn, he finds it necessary without the help of law, to rid the earth of an insidious and bloody villain. Already two of our friends, and one of them my own born brother, have perished in the enterprise. He himself, or I am much deceived, is taken in the same fatal toils. But at least he still lives and still hopes, as this billet sufficiently proves."

And the speaker, no other than Colonel Geraldine, proffered a letter, thus conceived:

"MAJOR HAMMERSMITH—On Wednesday, at 3 a.m., you will be admitted by the small door to the gardens of Rochester House, Regent's Park, by a man who is entirely in my interest. I must request you not to fail me by a second. Pray bring my case of swords, and, if you can find them, one or two gentlemen of conduct and discretion to whom my person is unknown. My name must not be used in this affair.

                                                    T. GODALL"

"From his wisdom alone, if he had no other title," pursued Colonel Geraldine, when the others had each satisfied his curiosity, "my friend is a man whose directions should implicitly be followed. I need not tell you, therefore, that I have not so much as visited the neighbourhood of Rochester House; and that I am still as wholly in the dark as either of yourselves as to the nature of my friend's dilemma. I betook myself, as soon as I had received this order, to a furnishing contractor, and, in a few hours, the house in which we now are had assumed its late air of festival. My scheme was at least original; and I am far from regretting an action which has procured me the services of Major O'Rooke and Lieutenant Brackenbury Rich. But the servants in the street will have a strange awakening. The house which this evening was full of lights and visitors they will find uninhabited and for sale tomorrow morning. Thus even the most serious councils," added the Colonel, "have a merry side."

"And let us add a merry ending," said Brackenbury.

The Colonel consulted his watch.

"It is now hard on two," he said. "We have an hour before us, and a swift cab is at the door. Tell me if I may count upon your help."

"During a long life," replied Major O'Rooke, "I never took back my hand from anything, nor so much as hedged a bet."

Brackenbury signified his readiness in the most becoming terms; and after they had drunk a glass or two of wine, the Colonel gave each of them a loaded revolver, and the three mounted into the cab and drove off for the address in question.

Rochester House was a magnificent residence on the banks of the canal. The large extent of the garden isolated it in an unusual degree from the annoyances of neighbourhood. It seemed the *parc aux cerfs* of some great nobleman or millionaire. As far as could be seen from the street, there was not a glimmer of light in any of the numerous windows of the mansion; and the place had a look of neglect, as though the master had been long from home.

The cab was discharged, and the three gentlemen were not long in discovering the small door, which was a sort of postern in a lane between two garden walls. It still wanted ten or fifteen minutes of the appointed time; the rain fell heavily, and the adventurers sheltered themselves below some pendent ivy, and spoke in low tones of the approaching trial.

Suddenly Geraldine raised his finger to command silence, and all three bent their hearing to the utmost. Through the continuous noise of the rain, the steps and voices of two men became audible from the other side of the wall; and, as they drew nearer, Brackenbury, whose sense of hearing was remarkably acute, could even distinguish some fragments of their talk.

"Is the grave dug?" asked one.

"It is," replied the other; "behind the laurel hedge. When the job is done, we can cover it with a pile of stakes."

The first speaker laughed, and the sound of his merriment was shocking to the listeners on the other side.

"In an hour from now," he said.

And by the sound of the steps it was obvious that the pair had separated, and were proceeding in contrary directions.

Almost immediately after, the postern door was cautiously opened, a white face was protruded into the lane, and a hand was seen beckoning to the watchers. In dead silence the three passed the door, which was immediately locked behind them, and followed their guide through several garden alleys to the kitchen entrance of the house. A single candle burned in the great paved kitchen, which was destitute of the customary furniture; and as the party proceeded to ascend from thence by a flight of winding stairs, a prodigious noise of rats testified still more plainly to the dilapidation of the house.

Their conductor preceded them, carrying the candle. He was a lean man, much bent, but still agile; and he turned from time to time and admonished silence and caution by his gestures. Colonel Geraldine followed on his heels, the case of swords under one arm and a pistol ready in the other. Brackenbury's heart beat thickly. He perceived that they were still in time; but he judged from the alacrity of the old man that the hour of action must be near at hand; and the circumstances of this adventure were so obscure and menacing, the place seemed so well chosen for the darkest acts, that an older man than Brackenbury might have been pardoned a measure of emotion as he closed the procession up the winding stair.

At the top the guide threw open a door and ushered the three officers before him into a small apartment, lighted by a smoky lamp and the glow of a modest fire. At the chimney corner sat a man in the early prime of life, and of a stout but courtly and commanding appearance. His attitude and expression were those of the most unmoved composure; he was smoking a cheroot with much enjoyment and deliberation, and on a table by his elbow stood a long glass of some effervescing beverage which diffused an agreeable odour through the room.

"Welcome," said he, extending his hand to Colonel Geraldine. "I knew I might count on your exactitude."

"On my devotion," replied the Colonel, with a bow.

"Present me to your friends," continued the first; and, when that ceremony had been performed, "I wish, gentlemen," he added, with the most exquisite affability, "that I could offer you a more cheerful programme; it is ungracious to inaugurate an acquaintance upon serious affairs; but the compulsion of events is stronger than the obligations of good-fellowship. I hope and believe you will be able to forgive me this unpleasant evening; and for men of your stamp it will be enough to know that you are conferring a considerable favour.

"Your Highness," said the Major, "must pardon my bluntness. I am unable to hide what I know. For some time back I have suspected Major Hammersmith, but Mr Godall is unmistakable. To seek two men in London unacquainted with Prince Florizel of Bohemia was to ask too much at Fortune's hands."

"Prince Florizel!" cried Brackenbury in amazement.

And he gazed with the deepest interest on the features of the celebrated personage before him.

"I shall not lament the loss of my incognito," remarked the Prince, "for it enables me to thank you with the more authority. You would have done as much for Mr Godall, I feel sure, as for the Prince of Bohemia; but the latter can perhaps do more for you. The gain is mine," he added, with a courteous gesture.

And the next moment he was conversing with the two officers about the Indian army and the native troops, a subject on which, as on all others, he had a remarkable fund of information and the soundest views.

There was something so striking in this man's attitude at a moment of deadly peril that Brackenbury was overcome with respectful admiration; nor was he less sensible to the charm of his conversation or the surprising amenity of his address. Every gesture, every intonation, was not only noble in itself, but seemed to ennoble the fortunate mortal for whom it was intended; and Brackenbury confessed to himself with enthusiasm that this was a sovereign for whom a brave man might thankfully lay down his life.

Many minutes had thus passed, when the person who had introduced them into the house, and who had sat ever since in a corner, with his watch in his hand, arose and whispered a word into the Prince's ear.

"It is well, Dr Noel," replied Florizel, aloud; and then addressing the others, "You will excuse me, gentlemen," he added, "if I have to leave you in the dark. The moment now approaches."

Dr Noel extinguished the lamp. A faint, grey light, premonitory of the dawn, illuminated the window, but was not sufficient to illuminate the room; and when the Prince rose to his feet, it was impossible to distinguish his features or to make a guess of the nature of the emotion which obviously affected him as he spoke. He moved towards the door, and placed himself at one side of it in all attitude of the wariest attention.

"You will have the kindness," he said, "to maintain the strictest silence, and to conceal yourselves in the densest of the shadow."

The three officers and the physician hastened to obey, and for nearly ten minutes the only sound in Rochester House was occasioned by the excursions of the rats behind the woodwork. At the end of that period, a loud creak of a hinge broke in with surprising distinctness on the silence; and shortly after, the watchers could distinguish a slow and cautious tread approaching up the kitchen stair. At every second step the intruder seemed to pause and lend an ear, and during these intervals, which seemed of an incalculable duration, a profound disquiet possessed the spirit of the listeners.

Dr Noel, accustomed as he was to dangerous emotions, suffered an almost pitiful physical prostration; his breath whistled in his lungs, his teeth grated one upon another, and his joints cracked aloud as he nervously shifted his position.

At last a hand was laid upon the door, and the bolt shot back with a slight report. There followed another pause, during which Brackenbury could see the Prince draw himself together noiselessly as if for some unusual exertion. Then the door opened, letting in a little more of the light of the morning; and the figure of a man appeared upon the threshold and stood motionless. He was tall, and carried a knife in his hand. Even in the twilight they could see his upper teeth bare and glistening, for his mouth was open like that of a hound about to leap. The man had evidently been over the head in water but a minute or two before; and even while he stood there the drops kept falling from his wet clothes and pattered on the floor.

The next moment he crossed the threshold. There was a leap, a stifled cry, an instantaneous struggle; and before Colonel Geraldine could spring to his aid, the Prince held the man, disarmed and helpless, by the shoulders.

"Dr Noel," he said, "you will be so good as to relight the lamp."

And relinquishing the charge of his prisoner to Geraldine and Brackenbury, he crossed the room and set his back against the chimney-piece. As soon as the lamp had kindled, the party beheld Florizel, the careless gentleman; it was the Prince of Bohemia, justly incensed and full of deadly purpose, who now raised his head and addressed the captive President of the Suicide Club.

"President," he said, "you have laid your last snare, and your own feet are taken in it. The day is beginning; it is your last morning. You have just swum the Regent's Canal; it is your last bathe in this world. Your old accomplice, Dr Noel, so far from betraying me, has delivered you into my hands for judgement. And the grave you had dug for me this afternoon shall serve, in God's almighty providence, to hide your own just doom from the curiosity of mankind. Kneel and pray, sir, if you have a mind that way; for your time is short, and God is weary of your iniquities."

The President made no answer either by word or sign; but continued to hang his head and gaze sullenly on the floor, as though he were conscious of the Prince's prolonged and unsparing regard.

"Gentlemen," continued Florizel, resuming the ordinary tone of his conversation, "this is a fellow who has long eluded me, but whom thanks to Dr Noel, I now have tightly by the heels. To tell the story of his misdeeds would occupy more time than we can now afford; but if the canal had contained nothing but the blood of his victims, I believe the wretch would have been no drier than you see him. Even in an affair of this sort I desire to preserve the forms of honour. But I make you the judges, gentlemen—this is more an execution than a duel; and to give the rogue his choice of weapons would be to push too far a point of etiquette. I cannot afford to lose my life in such a business," he continued, unlocking the case of swords; "and as a pistol bullet travels so often on the wings of chance, and skill and courage may fall by the most trembling marksman, I have decided, and I feel sure you will approve my determination, to put this question to the touch of swords."

When Brackenbury and Major O'Rooke, to whom these remarks were particularly addressed, had each intimated his approval, "Quick, sir," added Prince Florizel to the President, "choose a blade and do not keep me waiting; I have an impatience to be done with you for ever."

For the first time since he was captured and disarmed the President raised his head, and it was plain that he began instantly to pluck up courage.

"Is it to be stand up?" he asked eagerly, "and between you and me?"

"I mean so far to honour you," replied the Prince.

"Oh, come!" cried the President. "With a fair field, who knows how things may happen? I must add that I consider it handsome behaviour on your Highness's part; and if the worst comes to the worst I shall die by one of the most gallant gentlemen in Europe."

And the President, liberated by those who had detained him, stepped up to the table and began, with minute attention, to select a sword.

He was highly elated, and seemed to feel no doubt that he should issue victorious from the contest. The spectators grew alarmed in the face of so entire a confidence, and adjured Prince Florizel to reconsider his intention.

"It is but a farce," he answered; "and I think I can promise you, gentlemen, that it will not be long a-playing."

"Your Highness will be careful not to over-reach," said Colonel Geraldine.

"Geraldine," returned the Prince, "did you ever know me fail in a debt of honour? I owe you this man's death, and you shall have it."

The President at last satisfied himself with one of the

rapiers, and signified his readiness by a gesture that was not devoid of a rude nobility. The nearness of peril, and the sense of courage, even to this obnoxious villain lent an air of manhood and a certain grace.

The Prince helped himself at random to a sword.

"Colonel Geraldine and Dr Noel," he said, "will have the goodness to await me in this room. I wish no personal friend of mine to be involved in this transaction. Major O'Rooke, you are a man of some years and a settled reputation—let me recommend the President to your good graces. Lieutenant Rich will be so good as to lend me his attentions: a young man cannot have too much experience in such affairs."

"Your Highness," replied Brackenbury, "it is an honour I shall prize extremely."

"It is well," returned Prince Florizel; "I shall hope to stand your friend in more important circumstances."

And so saying he led the way out of the apartment and down the kitchen stairs.

The two men who were thus left alone threw open the window and leaned out, straining every sense to catch an indication of the tragical events that were about to follow. The rain was now over; day had almost come, and the birds were piping in the shrubbery and on the forest trees of the garden. The Prince and his companions were visible for a moment as they followed an alley between two flowering thickets; but at the first corner a clump of foliage intervened, and they were again concealed from view. This was all that the Colonel and the physician had an opportunity to see, and the garden was so vast, and the place of combat evidently so remote from the house, that not even the noise of sword-play reached their ears.

"He has taken him towards the grave," said Dr Noel, with a shudder.

"God," cried the Colonel, "God defend the right!"

And they awaited the event in silence, the Doctor shaking with fear, the Colonel in an agony of sweat. Many minutes must have elapsed, the day was sensibly broader, and the birds were singing more heartily in the garden before a sound of returning footsteps recalled their glances towards the door. It was the Prince and the two Indian officers who entered. God had defended the right.

"I am ashamed of my emotion," said Prince Florizel, "I feel it is a weakness unworthy of my station, but the continued existence of that hound of hell had begun to prey upon me like a disease, and his death has more refreshed me than a night of slumber. Look, Geraldine," he continued, throwing his sword upon the floor, "there is the blood of the man who killed your brother. It should be a welcome sight. And yet," he added, "see how strangely we men are made! my revenge is not yet five minutes old, and already I am beginning to ask myself if even revenge be attainable on this precarious stage of life. The ill he did, who can undo it? The career in which he amassed a huge fortune (for the house itself in which we stand belonged to him)—that career is now a part of the destiny of mankind for ever: and I might weary myself making thrusts in carte until the crack of judgement, and Geraldine's brother would be none the less dead, and a thousand other innocent persons would be none the less dishonoured and debauched. The existence of a man is so small a thing to take, so mighty a thing to employ! Alas!" he cried, "is there anything in life so disenchanting as attainment?"

"God's justice has been done," replied the Doctor. "So much I behold. The lesson, your Highness, has been a cruel one for me; and I await my own turn with deadly apprehension."

"What was I saying?" cried the Prince. "I have punished, and here is the man beside us who can help me to undo. Ah, Dr Noel! you and I have before us many a day of hard and honourable toil; and perhaps, before we have done, you may have more than redeemed your early errors."

"And in the meantime," said the Doctor, "let me go and bury my oldest friend."

And this (observes the erudite Arabian) *is the fortunate conclusion of the tale. The Prince, it is superfluous to mention, forgot none of those who served him in this great exploit; and to this day his authority and influence help them forward in their public career, while his condescending friendship adds a charm to their private life. To collect* (continues my author) *all the strange events which this Prince has played the part of Providence were to fill the habitable globe with books.*